THE DUKE AND I

Forever Yours Series

STACY REID

Edited by AuthorsDesigns

Cover design and formatting by AuthorsDesigns

Dusean, always and forever.

FREE OFFER

SIGN UP TO MY NEWSLETTER TO CLAIM YOUR FREE BOOK!

To claim your FREE copy of Wicked Deeds on a Winter Night, a delightful and sensual romp to indulge in your reading addiction, please click here.

Once you've signed up, you'll_be among the first to hear about my new releases, read excerpts you won't find anywhere else, and patriciate in subscriber's only giveaways and contest. I send out on dits once a month and on super special occasion I might send twice, and please know you can unsubscribe whenever we no longer zing.

Happy reading!

Stacy Reid

PRAISE FOR NOVELS OF STACY REID

"**Duchess by Day, Mistress by Night** is a sensual romance with explosive chemistry between this hero and heroine!"—*Fresh Fiction Review*

"From the first page, Stacy Reid will captivate you! Smart, sensual, and stunning, you will not want to miss **Duchess by Day, Mistress by Night**!"—*USA Today bestselling author Christi Caldwell*

"I would recommend **The Duke's Shotgun Wedding** to anyone who enjoys passionate, fast-paced historical romance."—*Night Owl Reviews*

"**Accidentally Compromising the Duke**—Ms. Reid's story of loss, love, laughter and healing is all that I look for when reading romance and deserving of a 5-star review."—*Isha C., Hopeless Romantic*

"**Wicked in His Arms**—Once again Stacy Reid has left me spellbound by her beautifully spun story of romance between two wildly different people."—*Meghan L., LadywithaQuill.com*

"**Wicked in His Arms**—I truly adored this story and while it's very hard to quantify, this book has the hallmarks of the great historical romance novels I have read!"—*KiltsandSwords.com*

"One for the ladies...**Sins of a Duke** is nothing short of a romance lover's blessing!"—*WTF Are You Reading*

"**THE ROYAL CONQUEST** is raw, gritty and powerful, and yet, quite unexpectedly, it is also charming and endearing."—*The Romance Reviews*

OTHER BOOKS BY STACY

Series Boxsets

Forever Yours Series Bundle (Book 1-3)

Forever Yours Series Bundle (Book 4-6)

Forever Yours Series Bundle (Book 7-9)

The Amagarians: Book 1-3

Sinful Wallflowers series

My Darling Duke

Her Wicked Marquess

Forever Yours series

The Marquess and I

The Duke and I

The Viscount and I

Misadventures with the Duke

When the Earl was Wicked

A Prince of my Own

Sophia and the Duke

The Sins of Viscount Worsley

An Unconventional Affair

Mischief and Mistletoe

A Rogue in the Making

The Kincaids

Taming Elijah

Tempting Bethany

Lawless: Noah Kincaid

Rebellious Desires series

Duchess by Day, Mistress by Night

The Earl in my Bed

Wedded by Scandal Series

Accidentally Compromising the Duke

Wicked in His Arms

How to Marry a Marquess

When the Earl Met His Match

Scandalous House of Calydon Series

The Duke's Shotgun Wedding

The Irresistible Miss Peppiwell

Sins of a Duke

The Royal Conquest

The Amagarians

Eternal Darkness

Eternal Flames

Eternal Damnation

Eternal Phoenyx

Single Titles

Letters to Emily

Wicked Deeds on a Winter Night

The Scandalous Diary of Lily Layton

CHAPTER 1

Bellview Manor, Chiswick, England 1818

It was the unhappiest news imaginable.

Elliot George Ashbrook, the ninth Duke of Hartford was about to marry or make an announcement of some sorts that he was ready to settle down. All the marriage-minded mammas of the season would be deliriously overjoyed, and then the hunt for who would secure such a worthy and estimable match would commence with genteel vigor. Society would be atwitter for months, and all the newspapers would write about this unprecedented move by the duke. For so long society had declared him a scoundrel, a rake of the first order.

Miss Emma Amelia Fitzgerald pressed a fist to her chest as if that would stop the sudden ache that settled heavily in her heart. Elliot was to find a bride. The hand that had been poised to knock on the door to the study lowered. She had to gather her composure before facing her brother and his guest. It would not do for the duke to see the sheen of tears in her eyes or the pain that must be evident on a face that many had declared to be expressive. After all, it had been she who had rejected his offers of marriage several years ago. Although she did not regret her decision and despite her current situation a small part of her dearly wished he would renew his addresses. He had not asked her again, and her pride, doubts, and fear had prevented her from approaching him. Years had passed, eight to be exact. And she had realized he must have accepted she was impaired and unmarriageable.

"I did not realize you'd hoped to settle down," her brother, Anthony Fitzgerald, said. "I thought you cherished your liberty greatly."

"I've decided it's time," Elliot drawled. "I am nine and twenty and not getting any younger. I'll signal my intention by attending Lady Wiles's ball in two weeks' time."

Elliot hadn't visited Bellview Manor in almost

six months. The duke's voice was richer and deeper, more confident than she remembered.

A rough sound of disbelief issued from her brother. "You are entirely serious. I cannot credit it. You have been a right rogue these last seasons. The polite world will be shocked and delighted. Do you have someone in mind?"

There was a contemplative pause.

"Perhaps Lady Andrea Sutton. She appears to be the most accomplished debutante of this season. I had the pleasure to dance with her last season and found her to be quite good-natured and intelligent."

"Not to mention stunningly beautiful and perfect."

Perfect. Everything Emma was not after the terrible carriage accident. The one her brother still blamed himself for because it had limited her prospects for marriage and a future. And because it had taken the man she loved…still loved if she was honest, the duke himself. Except when she had fallen hopelessly in love with him, he hadn't been a duke. They had been friends, neighbors, and everything then had seemed so simple, her place in the world defined and understood. Her expectations of marrying Elliot then and starting a family had been real and attainable, but in an instant, it had all been ripped away to be replaced by broken limbs and a hopeless heart. Her only solace was a change of scene, which she would achieve by travelling to Boston.

"Perfection is not a criterion of mine, but it does not hurt that she presents a very pretty picture."

There was a slight easing in her heart at that declaration.

Anthony said something she could not decipher, and she was so tempted to press her ear to the wooden panel. It was unforgivably rude to eavesdrop, but she consoled her conscience by recalling her need to gather composure before facing her brother and the duke. It pained her to admit even for a moment she wanted to retreat to the music room and resume playing the pianoforte. But she had never been a coward, and she would not start on this auspicious visit.

"Will I see you next week at Lady Waverly's house party?" Elliot asked.

Emma stiffened. That scandalous house party had been on the lips of many in society for weeks. The countess's yearly house party and her masquerade ball were notorious and only the rogues, the scoundrels, and the most scandalous women of the season attended. Though from what

Emma had gathered from the scandal sheets over the years, genteel ladies had donned masks and wigs to attend and had fallen to ruin.

"You know you won't find a wife there."

There was a low chuckle of masculine amusement. "That will be for pleasure," the duke drawled. "The countess's parties are always so amusing. I plan to indulge with a willing lady or two before I make my intentions to find a bride this season known."

A willing lady or two? The duke was indeed the worst sort of scoundrel. And her older brother's best friend. And the man she still loved with her entire soul.

"Why bother? You left the last masquerade without a lady on your arm, and the previous two before that if I recall correctly."

An annoyed grunt came from the duke. "There should be enough daring beauties to satisfy my discriminating tastes there this year."

The sound of glasses clinking echoed.

"How is Emma?"

Her heart shivered at the mention of her name.

"Still refusing to marry and insisting on taking an extended trip to America. I cannot imagine why she would want to visit that wild place."

The silence that lingered prompted her to lift her fist to knock on the door once more, but instead, she ran her hand over her light-blue, muslin, day dress smoothing non-existing wrinkles. She then took a deep breath and closed her eyes running a quick mental check over herself. Emma patted her stunning, bright red hair ensuring the artful chignon her maid had arranged had no loose wisps. She was in a presentable state to face him. She raised her hand to knock once again and paused as the duke's voice filtered through the door once more.

"You do not wish for her to leave?"

Was it her fanciful imagination that Elliot's voice sounded out of sorts?

"No, we all want to see her content in her own home with a husband and children. Father and I have discussed it. He will forbid her travelling."

Outrage snapped through Emma. Why did papa insist on ruling her life even though she was of age? It was not as if she were travelling to people who she knew nothing about. Her older sister, Elizabeth, had married an American business magnate and was blissfully settled in Boston. She had invited Emma over to meet their society, confident she would find some measure of happiness there. Though Emma doubted any such happiness would exist for her, she was thrilled with the notion of leaving England's shores for an extended period. Her family had not been happy to receive her news.

"What are her chances of making a respectable alliance?"

"At five and twenty? Little to none. There is something else," he muttered, sounding a trifle apprehensive. "Lord Coventry has declared his wish to marry her, and our father has agreed. Emma has no notion of the alliance."

Shock froze her. She had not heard of this outrage.

"Coventry! The man can't be a day under sixty." There was a thoughtful pause, and then the duke said, "Will she have him? You know she is very decided with her opinions."

"Deuced stubborn and fanciful, that's what she is."

"Still, the old earl cannot be acceptable. Emma will not be happy with your decision. Hell, I'm not happy with it," Elliot said gruffly, a vein of surprise in his tone.

"The task of arranging her a proper match is

harder than I'd imagined. She does not make it easy."

"You know it to be more. She is still hurt from…"

Her stomach knotted at the mention of her accident. Unable to tolerate the tone their discussion was taking, she knocked firmly and entered, moving carefully.

"Anthony dearest, I—" She paused, quite dramatically. "Your grace, I wasn't aware you had called."

Emma shifted to face him fully. She wasn't prepared for the impact of sensations upon seeing him. Pleasure and nerves. The duke's tall frame was one of powerful, lithe elegance. His dark hair was perfectly groomed, and his beautiful golden eyes ensnared her. His dark lashes were velveted soft and so long, she noticed as he bowed over her hand. His hands were strong and firm, and she was relieved when he let go of her fingers because the fleeting touch sent a thrill up her spine. Elliot was held to be driven and intense, reputed to be brilliant in business, a thing which had shocked society for a duke had no reason to be doing anything but being a duke. Even after eight years of mingling with the *ton*, Elliot was an enigma to both the press and society and unfortunately, a bit reserved and cold. Especially towards her.

Still, a frightening surge of longing and an ache travelled through her heart. He had only to be in the same room, and the response came unbidden.

The arrogant lift of his eyebrow and the amused slant of his lips said he knew her to be lying. Then his eyes dropped to her walking stick, and her gut tightened. It was always the first place someone looked, at the stick, and then her limp, and then pity would cross their features, and their voices would soften dramatically as if she were addled and they needed to speak with care.

How wretched it made her feel. Only a few people conversed with her without any undertones of pity and speculation.

"How wonderful to see you again, Miss Fitzgerald."

How formal he was, as if there hadn't been a time they had swum together in the pond, as if he hadn't taught her to fish, and as if he hadn't kissed her once, and stolen her heart away.

Relief filled her that he sounded normal, and his eyes had returned to her face. Not that he had ever treated her as an invalid, but it had been a while since they had cause to be in each other's company. She had never been able to predict his responses to her entirely. "It has been six months," she said pertly, wincing at the soft reprimand in her voice.

His expression was faintly amused. "Has it?"

His eyes were the deep gold of a lion, so stunning and unique. There had always been a profound stillness in his gaze, one that she felt she couldn't touch or understand, one that seemed to hold a thousand secrets. She'd always thought she was fanciful, unsure if the sensation of danger was real or an illusion. They stared at each other until her brother cleared his throat. She flushed and glanced away.

"Forgive me for interrupting you, Anthony. I've invited Vicar Marbury, his wife, and delightful daughter to dinner. I trust this is acceptable?"

Her brother scowled. "Do I have to be there? You know how Miss Marbury…she is too attentive."

Emma thought it served him right for being so odious in encouraging papa once again to select a husband for her, despite her stated wish not to marry. "I'm sure she'll be charming company." Emma faced Elliot. "Should I inform the housekeeper to set a place for you as well, Your Grace?"

"Regretfully I must decline. I have a previous engagement I cannot avoid."

"Of course." She gave him a small smile that felt too tight. "If I could speak with Anthony for a few minutes in privacy?"

"I was just about to take my leave," Elliot said smoothly. He dipped his head in a short bow and made his exit.

The door closed firmly on the duke's departure, and she made her way to the blue damask sofa and lowered herself, carefully arranging her walking stick to the side. She considered her brother for a few moments. It was mortifying to admit she had been eavesdropping, but she could not allow him and papa to decide her life as if she had no thoughts or hopes of her own.

Her family did nothing that did not administer to their own comfort, and it was evident they wanted her off their hands. A peculiar grief darted through her. "I've tried not to be a burden despite my limitations."

He shot her a reproving glance. "You are my sister, and I love you, Emma. You have never been a burden and never will be. You speak nonsense."

"Then why did you not tell me Papa was speaking with Lord Coventry about marriage? Is that not for your own comfort? For surely you could not believe I have any affection for the earl."

He raked his fingers through his hair. "I want what is best for you," he said with soft intensity. "Our family wants what is best for you."

"That would be allowing me to live my life however it makes me happy, Anthony."

"Do you not want a family, Emma? Children of your own."

A surge of longing darted through her heart, and a lump grew in her throat. She wanted a family, love, comfort, security, and happiness. She acknowledged the argument that she was like other women in wanting those things, but there was also an untapped desire that had brewed in her soul over the years. It had grown as she had come to terms with the fact that she was maimed. That part of her desired adventure, something different from the terrible predictability that was her life. Quite often the two needs mashed together painfully inside, disturbing any contentment she found with her current situation. Marrying Coventry when she did not love him, and when she would be the object of his pity and derision was not the sort of life she wanted. "Not with Coventry."

Her brother's brows came together in a considering frown. "He is only two and forty. He likes you despite…despite." He broke off with a frustrated growl.

Emma stood. "Despite my scars which he has not seen? Despite my limping? Despite that, on the days when the cramps are terrible, I use a wheelchair? Despite the fact I may truly never be able to have children? Did you or papa inform him of all the facts when he made his offer?"

His expression hardened. "He will call upon you tomorrow. I expect you to be courteous and give him a fair chance."

"I cannot promise to be available."

"You are unreasonable."

"I am not," she said firmly. "The last suitor you and papa pushed in my path informed me in no uncertain terms when we wed, I would remain in the country and never venture into society. I hadn't even accepted his offer, and he was ashamed of my situation. I cannot bear being trapped with anyone who would make me feel inferior and an object to be pitied. Can you assure me Lord Coventry would be different?"

Before her brother could reply, the door opened and in sailed their aunt Beatrice, who despite her short and plump stature, looked very elegant in a dark green riding habit, and matching hat with a decorative dyed feather. Bright blue eyes scanned the drawing room. "How delightful that you are both here! I've just arrived from Bath where I left your father and mother taking the waters. I've heard the wonderful news that Lord Coventry will be courting you. I thought you would need my guidance, my dear."

Exasperation rushed through Emma. "Not you too, Aunt Beatrice."

Her aunt shot her a bird-like look of inquiry. "But this is great news is it not?"

"No, it is not, I have no wish to be courted by Lord Coventry."

"But he is an earl!"

"My goodness, I'm a trifle tired. I am sure Anthony will explain." She ambled over to him and pressed a kiss to his cheek. "Thank you for caring, brother, but I do not need you to direct my life, just to love and support me."

Anthony scowled. "Emma—"

She walked away from his absurd orders, and her aunt's query of 'upon my word, have her senses departed her?' Emma moved out into the hallway, closing the door softly on her exit. Her family wanted her to be happy. She supposed one had to make allowances for that. But she would not let them dictate her life when she was of age, and had an inheritance of five thousand pounds and could manage her affairs herself. They evidently thought her an invalid and were willing to foist her onto the first man who showed some interest in her.

Except for Elliot…

Her throat tightened with remembered pain and happiness.

The acquaintance between herself and the duke had been longstanding, except he hadn't been the powerful and arrogant duke of Hartford then, merely the charming, good-natured, and ambitious Mr. Elliot Winthrop.

She was the second daughter of a gentleman, the Viscount Sherwood, and Elliot was the son of the local doctor. He'd always treated her with kindness and pleasant sweetness, never objecting as her brother had done when she insisted on riding astride in breeches with them across the fens or swimming in the lake in her chemisette, their laughter ringing across windswept grasslands. He hadn't thought her improper or ill-bred as her brother had often lamented, but had merely encouraged her to be daring and true to her own nature.

She had been fifteen at the time, to Elliot's nineteen, and had been quite desperately in love with her brother's friend. She had known without a doubt he was the man she would marry and had believed he felt a similar attachment.

Life had seemed happy, then the curricle race had happened, and everything had been unbearable for months. When Elliot had asked her to marry him while she lay hurt in bed, with pity in his eyes, she had said no for she had loved him too much to saddle him with a broken wife. He'd asked again, and she'd said no. She'd cared deeply that the two doctors her papa had consulted with, had declared the possibility of her never walking or having children because of her injuries. Her family had objected most passionately for he'd had no connections and wealth and had aspired to visit Edinburgh to study and become a doctor like his father. That aspect hadn't mattered to Emma though. He had renewed his offer several times over the next few months, and she had refused until he had stopped asking.

Then a few months later what had seemed like

an army of solicitors and the Duchess of Hartford had tracked him down to Devon. Her Elliot had been the next in line for a dukedom.

'Don't forget me,' she'd whispered fervently when he had been collected by the duchess whom Emma had dubbed the dragon.

'Will you…remember me?' she had asked with such aching sadness.

He'd given her a brief, wordless nod. Instead of walking away he stood for a timeless moment. "Wait for me, promise."

Her heart had soared with gladness. "I will," she'd replied, though knowing in her heart once he glimpsed the world before him, he wouldn't care to remember the broken daughter of an impoverished viscount. Eager to keep her promise to Elliot, she had written to him often, but he had been an indifferent correspondent, only replying to a few of the dozens of letters she had posted to him.

Of course, he had become imminently suitable to her family after it was confirmed he was the next duke of Hartford.

And now he was about to announce to polite society his intention to take a wife.

Emma made her way down the quiet hall at an unhurried pace. She paused at the bottom of the stairs, resting her head briefly on the banister. Why did her heart feel so laden with grief and regrets? It had taken years before she had been able to imagine a future without Elliot. She'd already made plans for her life, and she would see them through. If only before she left for America, she could dance with him, just once, or perhaps even kiss him, and perhaps just a bit more.

The thought arrested her.

What if…?

And suddenly she knew. Before she departed the shores of England, before she lost him forever, she would have one moment of sin, of stolen pleasure, and irresistible passion.

Instead of ascending the stairs, she made her way to the music room where her younger sister Maryann played the pianoforte. Emma entered, and her sister glanced up.

"Oh dear, you have *that* rebellious look in your eyes."

"I need your help, and I only have a week to prepare."

"Of course, whatever you need," she said with all the loyalty of a sister who loved her dearly.

She would attend Lady Waverly's house party,

or better, the masquerade ball customarily held at its conclusion. "We will have to be *very* discreet."

Maryann's eyes widened, and one of her hand fluttered to her chest. "Oh, dear."

Emma would avail herself of its advantages, namely pursuing a sensual encounter with the duke of Hartford. The very idea was positively indecent, shocking, and scandalous, but there was a chance to experience something that she'd always wanted.

Emma could only hope afterward she would not be left in ruined disgrace.

CHAPTER 2

Elliot George Winthrop, the ninth duke of Hartford had made time to take afternoon tea every Tuesday with his grandmother, the Duchess of Hartford, for almost eight years, and he could not recall if he had ever seen her display an expression of shock, or pleasure for that matter. It was remarkable that he couldn't remember if a smile had ever appeared on her lips.

As it were, the teacup was arrested half way to her lips. "I beg your pardon?"

"I've decided it is time for me to find a duchess."

His grandmother was now little more than a flesh covered skeleton, although her snow-white hair was impeccably styled under a Brussels lace cap, which Elliot knew must have cost a pretty penny. She was dressed in lavender silk trimmed with black ribbon bows, which denoted half mourning although her elder son had been dead eight years. She lowered the cup to the small and elegantly designed table before her. She gripped her walking cane, her bony fingers curling like claws over the head of the cane positioned at her front, and lion gold eyes, very much like his, stared at him assessing his reasons.

"And what has brought this on?"

"You've stalwartly impressed on me for years that it is my duty to the title since you restored me to my proper place," he said repeating the very words she had used over and over. He managed to keep his tone from revealing a trace of irony or sarcasm.

Elliot had decided to marry and had never had an aversion to the state. He wanted to do it now because he'd been feeling restless, dissatisfied with business, the social whirl of the *ton*, and the usual debaucheries and activities in which he had indulged for the last several years. He had found himself of late, yearning for the simple life he had left behind.

She is going to America soon…

He felt impatient, mostly with himself, for being stuck on Miss Emma Fitzgerald.

His grandmother's back straightened, and her jaw tightened. "I do not believe that for a minute. Have you gotten someone with child?"

A startled laugh escaped him. "No, madam. I am very careful in that regard, and I must say I find it decidedly inappropriate to have a discussion with you about my conquests."

She shot him a reproving glare. "Then what has brought on this decision?"

"I'm simply interested in a finding a woman who I would grow to love and have children with."

She regarded him with a most unpleasant expression. "Do not be foolish," she snapped, her eyes glaring her disapproval. "Love has no place within a marriage alliance. That useless emotion has been the downfall of many fine families. I do hope I have taught you better than that."

"Love is essential to me. My parents were devoted to each other. I admire and yearn for the kind of attachment they had."

The duchess's eyes grew chilled as they often did at the mention of his father, her second son who had dared run away to pursue his passion by becoming a doctor and then had the awful gall to fall in love with a lowly vicar's daughter. She had never forgiven him and had only deigned to acknowledge Elliot's father when her eldest son had died without issue, and worse, with the dukedom on the brink of financial ruin.

The dowager's lips pressed together for a moment before she said with icy imperiousness, "You will not repeat George's mistake. You'll select a lady from an estimable family, with a dowry fit for a duke, and in possession of a reputation that has never had a hint of scandal attached to it. I will only give my stamp of approval then."

George. Even the name of his father on her tongue seemed strange. She had cut him from all aspects of her heart and always left the room when Elliot tried to share stories of his family and how happy his father had been with his mother. It was as if she resented the very notion that he could have been contented away from the wealth and privilege of being born to a duke and duchess.

The first time he had mentioned in polite company that his father had been the local doctor of their village, she'd almost had apoplexy. Elliot didn't believe she had quite forgiven him for that *faux pas* nor had she ever ceased to deplore that it was his business acumen which had rescued them from financial ruin. He would leave an inheritance to his heir of which he had reason to be proud. He had been unprepared for the duties that came with the title, but he had never been the sort for flinching away from responsibility and hard work. Those business dealings supplemented the somewhat meager widow's pension she formerly had to keep her household. With the dukedom in debt, she had not been too proud to accept his plebeian earnings to pay her own debts. Nor had she sniffed at his offer to give her an additional allowance to make her life easier.

"My father loved my mother, it was never a mistake when he defied conventions to follow his heart and passion," he said mildly. "If you had witnessed their contentment with their lot in life, I daresay you would have thought the same."

"You disappoint me," she said, her voice low. "I do hope you are not thinking of approaching Viscount Sherwood's cripple—"

The delicate handle of his teacup snapped, and he shot her an icy glance. "I do not care who you are, you will be civil if not in thoughts, at least in speech and manners always concerning Miss Fitzgerald."

His grandmother's lips parted, but she did not speak.

"If she would have me, I would take her to be my wife, my duchess within a heartbeat, but it is she who will not have me." And he had too much pride and dignity to ever approach Emma for her hand in marriage again.

"She is not acceptable," the duchess said coldly.

"If you will excuse me, grandmother, I have business matters to attend," he said with icy politeness and stood.

"Impertinent." Her lips formed in a moue of distaste, as she had always done whenever he implied he worked. How it had confounded him in those early days when she'd ordered him to abandon those unworthy pursuits, and as duke, he need not lower himself so. Elliot had thought it ludicrous and continued with his investments and business holdings to her distress. How she had loathed that it was those investments that had made the dukedom solvent once more.

He made his way from the drawing room without further ado. It made no sense for him to even kiss her cheeks in adieu, she had never displayed any warmth towards him. Elliot truly fully understand why his father had run away from this life, and hidden the connection even whilst he lay dying. He had been there, holding his father's hand when he had taken his last breath, and he never mentioned he was the son of a duke, and that Elliot had another family elsewhere. The relationship had been filled with such acrimony and disappointment, his father had preferred for Elliot to think he was alone. He had lost his mother only two years before his father, and they had never been blessed with another child.

Those days had been filled with grief, the only hope and the little warmth he'd had in his life had come from his friendship with the honorable Anthony Fitzgerald. He hadn't allowed a distinction of rank to mar their friendship. Not that Elliot could say the same for Anthony's parents, they had always had a thin veneer of courtesy when they spoke with him, and he had been quite conscious he had not entirely belonged to their world. And also, there was Emma…

A pounding ache went through his heart, and he swiftly buried the pain. He would not think of her, not now, now when it had taken him so long to accept that she was not for him and never would be.

She had kept him at a distance with the pain and sadness in her eyes, the refusals on her tongue, and her determination not to see him in the early days after her accident. He had believed she thought him unworthy of her as the daughter of a viscount, but that he could not credit for she had never treated him as inferior before. He'd then surmised it was her parents' influence, but their entire manner towards him had decidedly changed when he was revealed to be the heir to the dukedom of Hartford.

You ask in vain, for I'll never consent to marry you… you, Elliot, deserve so much more than a cripple for a wife.

He hadn't been able to dent her surety that he would come to resent her. Elliot had wept with her when she had told him the doctors said she'd never walk again, but he had still wanted her to be his wife. His admiration hadn't dimmed, she, however, had maintained an air of civil friendship, even in the many letters she had written to him. There was no longer a sense of romance, the invitation to courtship, which had led him to risk the chance of kissing her lips. A decision he had relished and regretted in equal measures since their current state, for the memory of it haunted him too much.

But avoiding her had proved to be easy, for she was never in society. Whether it was her choice or not, he would never know, even though he understood it. The polite world had no use for broken things. Everything had to be pretty and perfect and estimable for them to find worth. All the unpretty things, the broken things, and the inestimable were discarded.

Instead of heading to his studies, he made his way outdoors and toward the large lake toward the eastern section of his estate. Glenhaven was a majestic building set in perfectly landscaped grounds. The frontage of the manor was Palladian in style although it covered a building that had been started in Elizabethan times. Hartford had not been a dukedom in those days, the family had risen under King James although the reasons for the gift of the title was another matter that his grandmother sought to avoid discussing. The estates had been somewhat rundown and neglected when he first became Duke, but now looked well-tended and profitable which Elliot was pleased to admit was true.

Picking up a few stones, he skipped them across the waters of the lake admiring the ripples on the surface. It was going to be a long night. He would not sleep. There was no sense in trying. Not when he had just seen Miss Emma Fitzgerald. Hauntingly lovely, enticingly exquisite and with her large sad eyes. For tonight, tomorrow, the day after that, and then even the next day he would dream of her, crave to kiss and touch, and then the need would fade, he hoped. That always happened, and it was one of the reasons he had avoided their country home, Bellview Manor for it would mean subjecting himself to the torment of wanting her, and knowing it was never to be.

EMMA WAS on the verge of doing something truly wicked.

She thought such an acknowledgment would fill her with dread. Instead, fevered anticipation sifted through her body as she slipped dark-apple-red dancing slippers onto her feet. She ran a fingertip over the straps crisscrossing her ankle, enjoying the supple feel of the delicate material.

"Are you quite certain?"

The soft question from Maryann, had nerves erupting inside Emma. "I am more certain than I have ever been. I need to do this, so I do not spend the rest of my years filled with abject regret. I already have more than I can bear. I promise you Elliot will not know it is me, and it will be only for tonight," she reassured Maryann with a smile, though nervousness knotted Emma's stomach.

"You must perceive the advantages of an eligible marriage. A union with Lord Coventry would render you a countess. You'd have a far greater allowance than I do, surely a carriage of your own, and you will be the mistress of your own home. Tonight…tonight if you do all I am thinking, you will render yourself unmarriageable."

"I do not wish to marry the earl. Everything else I can acquire with my inheritance from my grandmother." She cleared her throat. "And you forget I may not be able to bear issue."

"The doctors also said you would never walk again, Emma, and here you are."

Here you are. How simple it made the painful years of screaming and struggling to walk, the agony when her legs would fold beneath her, and the horror that would ice through her stomach as her leg muscles knotted and cramped. How she had fought and cried against her parents' orders to not walk but to stay in bed and use a Bath chair. They had even taken her stick, hating that she hurt herself with every effort it took to try and stand.

And it was for that very reason she would be directed only by her own desires, for if she had not clawed, prayed and pleaded with God, fought her parents and even Anthony, she would still be imprisoned by her infirmities. Life offered no certainties, and for once she was prepared to live on the dangerous edge she had admired others for living on.

Elliot would soon be married, and she would soon be on another continent. They might never meet again, and she would forever dream of him. Unless she took a memory of him when she left, and not just any memory would do, something sweet, and passionate, and something wonderful. That stark, blinding truth had been whipping through her mind for almost a week now, and she had done everything possible to prepare for tonight. She would have one chance to experience something…anything with Elliot, before she walked away from everything she had ever wanted and known she would never have.

The thrill of something positively improper, unexpected and wicked had tingled along her spine. She needed this, not just to taste passion with her duke, but to step from the cage her family had designed and kept her in for years. *I am five and twenty.* By all accounts a spinster, and unmarriageable, even without her scars and limitations. There were only a few options available to women in her position. She could wait…wait to die, wait to live…or she could act.

Emma had decided to act.

She just wasn't sure how to make her sister understand the driving force behind her decision. Maryann had been questioning Emma's sanity since she'd confided her too daring plans.

Maryann reclined in the chaise longue, her hand rubbing her well-rounded stomach. "How I wish you a happiness like mine," she said with a sigh. "I confess I do not wish for you to leave us, I am quite attached to you my dear Emma, and you will miss the arrival of your niece or nephew." She pursed her lips. "I am nervous Papa or Anthony will discover. I have observed that Papa can be frightful in his anger at times."

Her sister was right; Emma was petrified. Not because her brother or papa might discover her recklessness. But that she would fail to rouse Elliot's interest, and had to endure a lifetime of regrets, like never kissing him again or holding him for more than a few seconds. It had been distressing to realize how empty her life was, and how fearful she was to act on the hope and desires she'd harbored for years.

There was no joy at the thought of being a countess, only a raw, unbridled fear that a lifetime with someone she held no affections for would reflect her parents' indifferent relationship. That he would treat her with pity and disdain because of her wounds.

She wanted to break away and be free, even if for only one night. She felt suffocated, and the need for something else had been roiling inside her. A seething cauldron of restlessness, hope, and need for more. One night for herself to indulge and she only wanted that with Elliot, the boy she had loved with such intensity, and the man she still admired, if only because of his business acumen and charitable kindness, for he did not allow her close enough for anything else. Perhaps if she had one wicked night with the duke, she could move on from him, and just maybe finally silence the part of her that had started longing for him since her fifteenth year. She'd always struggled with wicked unladylike thoughts of Elliot kissing her, and doing so much more.

I'll not trouble you with my unwanted sentiments ever again, Miss Emma. And he had been faithful to his words, even when she had silently cried and hoped he would not give up on her.

"Are you not at all scared. What if…what if your leg…"

Dark emotions reared its head and clogged her throat. There were days she wished she was as unblemished as her sister. If that were so, she wouldn't be so nervous about seducing someone as handsome and self-assured as Elliot. "I will be fine. I've taken long walks through the gardens without my walking stick. And I am wearing stockings. I shan't remove them at all."

"Emma, how scandalous are you hoping to be?" Her sister demanded in a horrified whisper, her light blue eyes flashing with excitement and trepidation.

"I plan to be as scandalous as possible. Isn't that the objective of a masquerade at a country manor? Debauchery and wickedness?" Emma could not tell if she was expectant or terrified.

Her sister lightly touched her hand. "Oh, Emma, I wish I were brave as you."

Emma smiled and smoothed her hand over the soft lines of her dress. She wore a dark red satin gown with a dubious neckline. The depth of the décolletage was more revealing than Emma had ever dared wear before, but it was modest compared with those her sister had worn since her marriage. This was not a gown that would be considered suitable for an unwed virgin lady. It invited male interest and definitely suggested that interest would be encouraged. Emma had a tiny waist and had daringly decided not to wear her stays under the dress, so the gown revealed the actual contours of her body not just the delicate flesh of her voluptuous breasts. It had taken her all week with the help of Maryann to complete the gown. "Do I pass muster?"

"Oh Emma, you are gorgeous." A blush heated Maryann's face, and she rubbed her pregnant belly almost absently. "Do you…do you know what will happen? Though I am younger, I am a married woman, and you have no notion what to expect in a seduction."

Emma's entire body blushed when she understood her sister's apparent mortification. "He has kissed me before…it was years ago."

"I gather you plan to do far more than kissing," Maryann said pertly, her face burning a brighter red.

"I…if the situation calls for it."

"I cannot credit I am about to tell you how to prepare for a scoundrel to take liberties with you!"

Emma choked back a horrified laugh. "It is not

necessary, I am sure Elliott knows how to take liberties with a woman," she said softly, though she desperately wished she knew. "The carriage is ready, and I must leave and return before Anthony reaches home."

"You do know if he is likely to be there?"

A shiver, half dread, half anticipation, ruffled her nerves.

"I believe he said he had a previous engagement and would not attend the masquerade. And even if he does, he is quite unlikely to recognize me with this blonde wig and face mask, and without my walking stick. You needn't worry, Maryann, all shall be well."

"We have never done anything quite so scandalous, and I've been told by mamma my marriage to Dr. Hugh Grantham bordered on indecency. If this ever becomes known, I daresay you will send mamma to an early grave."

"I do not want to live with regrets, Maryann, I do not want to look back on my life twenty years from now and wonder what it would have been like to just be with him," she said softly. "To kiss him, even if it is just once more."

A tingle of excitement jolted through her system. No one else had ever stirred this raw sensuality inside of her, the one that roiled in her blood, screaming for freedom.

"Promise me you will be careful. Our brother must never know, Emma."

"I cannot live under the thumb of Anthony in every aspect of my life. I already feel as if I am a shadow of who I could be."

The tide of familiar pain and regret rose to choke her like thick smoke. She needed this, or one day she would simply shatter, and nothing would be able to piece her back together.

Tonight, she would live.

CHAPTER 3

Every sense and emotion of Elliot narrowed onto the lady who sauntered into the grand ballroom of the Lady Waverly's stately country manor. He froze, but just for a moment. *Miss Emma Fitzgerald.* He would know the curve of her lips, that pointed chin, and her delectably petite shape and curves anywhere. His foundation rocked at the implication she was at Lady Waverly's house party and masquerade ball. These sorts of entertainment were ones no genteel lady of society should attend. The lack of a limp surprised him. Since the accident, he had never encountered her before without a cane for assistance. *Perhaps I am mistaken in the identity*. It was unpardonable that someone else could elicit such a visceral reaction in him.

A mass of silky dark blonde strands was piled atop her head in an elaborate style. Clearly, a wig, for Miss Emma Fitzgerald was the possessor of a mane of glorious red hair that burned like fire under the sun. Her lips were painted vixen red, luscious and pouting. Her sensual body was fitted into a red ball gown with a distressingly lowered neckline, which hugged along her breasts like a possessive lover, before falling in a shimmer to her ankles. The cut of the gown accented her small waist and all her generous curves. The domino mask was one of dark gold with black feathers, fashioned to cover the upper part of her cheeks and nose.

No…it was her, and a fierce dart of pride arrowed through him at her accomplishment. How he wished she had allowed him to be there for her through what must have been dark and trying times.

Something he had thought long dead rose from the silent depths of his soul. It stirred, stretched, and hummed as a blast of pleasure rocked him back on his heels. Emma was *here*, in his domain.

Devil take it. *Why is she here?*

It should be patently obvious to his scrambled brain, but somehow, he couldn't process that Emma was dressed so provocatively, or worse she had planned a tryst. There was truly no other reason to attend the countess's yearly ball *but* to be scandalous. There were no debutants here, no charming ingénues, only rakes and scoundrels, Cyprians, merry widows, disenchanted wives, courtesans and their debauchers. He watched her covertly from the upper balcony of the second floor, a dark and secluded spot covered by jungle like greenery where he had been lingering and watching the rowdy throng below. A worried frown flittered over her features, and her teeth bit her lower lip betraying her nervousness. *That wide lush mouth.* He'd imagined kissing them, at first gently, then ravenously, for years.

Being so focused on her lips, it took him a few seconds to realize she searched for someone specifically. He would call out and put a bullet in whoever she planned to rendezvous with. Elliot would not allow a bounder to take advantage of her sweetness, her innocence, and the lush sensuality with which she glowed.

He almost sent a note to Anthony who had elected to attend a ball in London and decided against it. Emma would be more than embarrassed if Elliot informed her brother of her recklessness. It was not as if she was a young debutante anymore. She was five and twenty. He convinced himself he was only doing what any friend of Anthony's would do as Elliot followed her, working his way down the winding stairs, always a few paces behind her, never letting her out of his sight as she made her way through the crowded ballroom.

Boredom no longer held him. All ennui had vanished the moment he spied her. It was a dangerous thing to acknowledge. He wanted to gut the men that enjoyed a double, triple, a quadruple glance and salivated despite being with their own ladies. He would know exactly where to cut, he thought viciously, for he had assisted his father numerous times in his surgery.

Emma was alluring, but it was more than that. The lush eroticism she displayed with her sweet voluptuous body drew every libertine's unabashed admiration. But it would be the innocence that sparkled from her dark blue eyes that enticed. It shouldn't, but it did. The predator in the men around would soon stir, and the dark primal part of them would itch to take her untapped sensuality and corrupt her. *That* was certainly the effect she had on him. Elliot wanted to wrap those wide sexy pouting lips of hers around his cock, bruising and pleasuring her lips, and then ride her body for hours.

Bloody Hell.

Anger snapped through him, and he gritted his teeth against his lurid thoughts. What the hell was wrong with him? This was the reason he had stayed so faithfully away from Emma. He was unable to conceal his evident desire for her, and he had gained a broken nose to prove the consequences of thinking carnally about her.

After a few minutes of casually circling the packed ballroom, her shoulders wilted. The confidence she had strolled in with wavered, and she spun as if heading for the entrance then faltered.

He frowned, concern curling through him as she clearly battled with herself. Whatever it was she fought with, the determination won. She visibly firmed her shoulders, notched her chin a little higher and sauntered back into the throng. A few gentlemen wasted no time approaching her, and while she smiled and responded, he could see her wariness.

A servant was passing with a tray of champagne, she reached out and snared a glass.

Why was she there? Why would she take such a

risk with her reputation? No one attended Lady Waverly's masquerade ball for dancing and fun, they sought illicit pleasures and discreet bedding partners. Lady Waverly might have gained a title from her marriage to the late Peregrine Chambers, Earl of Waverly but she was not truly part of society. She reigned over London's *demi-mondaine*, but she would always be thought of as a former high-class courtesan who had caught her aging husband in parson's mousetrap. If her luscious charms had driven the old man to his grave early, as was rumored, then he had departed the earth with a smile on his face. However, much of the old tabbies of the *ton* deplored her existence, she had provided her earl with an heir and a spare before he headed for pastures new.

Elliot leaned against a column, careful to be out of her line of sight and observed how Emma behaved. She was looking for someone, and that man had not long to live, for Elliot would make sure the bastard failed in seducing her. She stood out from the crowd in a manner that was both alarming and enticing. Surely the predatory rakes would detect the innocent within their mix and want to be the first to seduce her into bed. She also wore the least revealing gown, the barely-there décolletage designed to entice, and from the admiring glances aimed her way, she had certainly succeeded.

She stood apart from the fashionable crowd, a small smile on that wide lush mouth as she observed the dancers. Beautifully gowned, and bejeweled women were gliding around the room in a waltz, and they were being held far too close than was considered appropriate. But that was the point, here they could be as scandalous as they wanted without judgment, safe behind their masks and wigs.

It was one of the reasons he liked attending Lady Waverly's outrageous parties and balls. It was the one night people were honest with their needs and desires. Here the rules of modesty and decorum, duplicity and pretentiousness were forgotten once everyone alighted from their carriages. Here ladies and gentlemen were far bolder and more improper than they might have been otherwise. It was so unusual for people to be themselves in the world he had been thrust in. Elliot hoped the day would eventually come when everyone would do away with the masks and be themselves without fear of judgement.

Emma seemed undecided, and her evident nervousness grew, and after the third glass of champagne, she seemed jittery. A few gentlemen sidled up to her, and with wide eyes, she shook her head wordlessly. One lingered, the persistent bounder, but with a sweet smile, she left the presence of Viscount Beauford and strolled along the edge of the ballroom.

And not once did Elliot remove his gaze from Emma. *He had missed her.*

Though he had seen her last week, he hadn't taken the time to converse with her. Her face had lighted with pleasure when she had seen him, and some of his loneliness had been chased away. It was damned stupid, but her smile always had that effect on him. Warmth crept inside when she bestowed it in his direction, intentionally or not. Elliot didn't even want to think about the power of her laugh, or he might do something stupid. Something like thinking her presence at the scandalous house party meant more, meant that he could satisfy whatever craving drove her here.

She exited the ballroom and walked with slow, measured steps down the massive hallway. He lingered in the shadowed entrance of the ballroom until he noted where she went. A few minutes later she emerged from the withdrawing room and walked back toward the main staircase. She went through the French door and into a small, secluded garden. A part of him knew he would regret it, but he was compelled to ensure her safety. Though in his gut, Elliot knew the person she needed protection from most was himself.

A soft breeze whispered through the trees, carrying with it the scent of jasmine and roses. She lifted her face to the cool night air, and the sigh that issued from her was forlorn. Emma moved further into the gardens, skirting pass a birdbath with surprising grace. Elliot made his way over to the lone fountain and lowered himself onto a stone bench which was partially obscured by an over pruned rosebush. He must have made some sound, for she whipped around with more speed and grace than he'd expected. Her eyes flicked around the shadows of the garden, probing and seeking. He stood, and stepped closer, their gazes collided, and she swallowed. The movement was slight, and if Elliot hadn't been watching her so intently, he would have missed it. What he saw in her blue gaze froze him—relief, a hot flash of desire and need, before her lids shuttered.

Sweet mercy!

He gripped his glass of whisky, needing an anchor, and lifted the glass to his lips, and with one long swallow finished his drink, his gaze never leaving her body. She momentarily looked away, then a few beats later glanced back at him and smiled. His awareness of her became acute and intense. *Too intense.* She finished her glass of champagne in one swallow, set it down by the birdbath, and glided across the expanse of the lawns her stride so confident and sensual he was magnetized. There was no limp, no evident discomfort and for a moment he wondered if it had been his fevered dreams why he had thought this lady was Emma. She sauntered toward him, and he was unable to glance away from her exquisitely voluptuous figure, the sway of her hips, and the determination in her walk.

Sensations skittered across Elliot's nerve endings. His breath seized when he realized little Emma was on the prowl—for *him*. The knowledge filled him with stark need, and fear, and damn if it would abate. He slowly sat, needing something firmer than the ground beneath him. She reached his darkened corner and stepped between his casually splayed legs.

"They say you are the man to see when one wants to indulge in sin," she said with a low husky voice that trembled slightly.

His heart was damned well near to bursting from his chest. *What?* "Do they?"

"Are you not the duke of Hartford, the gentleman dubbed for the last several seasons as a veritable rake of the first order, London's wickedest lover, and society's most devilish duke?"

The question caused his stomach to tighten. "Not everything printed in the scandal sheet is true." He'd only had a few lovers, and he was quite discriminating when selecting those lovers. He did not dally with innocents, nor had he ever bedded a married or affianced lady.

"So, I've been misinformed. A pity," she drawled, effortlessly captivating his interest when all the other ladies for this season had been unable to do so. But then Emma Fitzgerald had always been his weakness.

"Well, half of it is true."

"The better part?"

"The dangerous half."

Her lips curved in approval.

"You must tell me your name so I won't be at a disadvantage," he said, beyond curious as to her response. Lady Waverly had designed her masquerade so only the identities of the ladies, who had far more to lose within society, were protected.

"A lady intrigued by the decadence and notorious vices a masquerade ball offers."

The silence that stretched between them was filled with something dangerous and exciting.

He almost expired on the spot. "How intrigued?"

She made no reply. Instead, she stepped between Elliot's splayed legs, brushing against his thighs. *Bold.* Oh so bold and unlike Emma. He tried to reason around the hum of need firing his brain cells. It was then he noticed the mask was not a mask at all but gold paint. Somehow, she had used makeup like the actors did on stage, and whatever else he couldn't imagine, painting the mask onto her face. The painting covered her forehead, nose, and top half of her cheeks in dark shades of gold. Only the shape of her eyes was fitted with an elegant apple red and black mask that curved to her ears.

"You are beautiful," he whispered.

Her eyes widened, her lips parted, but she did not speak.

Unable to halt the desire, he allowed the tips of his fingers to trail along the line of her neck to the hollow of her shoulder. She did not slap his cheeks or flounce away. *Good God.* What else would she permit?

He lowered his hand, thinking furiously. There was no doubt it was *her*. Everything about Emma had been imprinted on his heart. Her scent. The shape and texture of her body. Her laugh, and that low growl she made when she was angry. Never for a moment had he doubted it. He might not have seen her often over the last two years, but everything about Emma had been indelibly seared into his mind. The smooth huskiness of her voice, her lush sensuality, the shy peeks she tended to give him from beneath her lashes, and her laugh. *God, her laugh*. Low, husky, yet utterly feminine. Why was she truly at this house party which was designed for sin and debauchery? A slight smile lingered on her lips, but he could see the nervousness and the impossible lust. His cock hardened on a surge of need so painful his hands trembled. He released the tight clamp on his glass, setting it on the fountain's ledge, and stuffed his offending appendages deep in his trousers and tried to convince himself to turn her away.

She was his best friend's younger sister. She was a lady, and she was an innocent. She was off limits to him.

"Tell me your name."

She licked her bottom lip, a nervous habit her mother constantly scolded her for.

"No names," she breathed huskily.

"Tell me," he said with more force than he'd intended.

"I'm Amelia, Your Grace." She dipped into a quick, graceful curtsy, and smiled, which wobbled at his lack of response.

Amelia? Her middle name? How could she not fathom he knew everything there was to know about her?

"A pleasure, Amelia. Let's not be formal, please, call me Elliot," he said slowly, wondering what the hell he was doing.

"Elliot," she said softly as if tasting his name. "A pleasure."

"Why are you here?" Perhaps she would think the question odd, giving the nature of the ball, and the evident reason people attended. He waited for her reply with patience that impressed him.

"I've always enjoyed gardens," she said with a twinkle in her eyes, alerting him that she was deliberately obtuse.

She glanced toward the revelry. "This ball is more thrilling than how I imagined it. It is elegant yet pulses with a raw undertone of danger. It's beautiful."

Her eyes were direct as they probed his in the shadows. "I have always wanted to explore a night of sin, and the countess's spring ball is famous for showing its patrons a great time."

After the briefest of hesitation, she continued, "Would you like to go someplace quiet?"

He drew in a swift breath at her teasing, and far too enticing suggestion, his heart ceased beating. He was sure it took a few seconds before it started to move in his chest. But he had heard right. Emma had just given him one of the oldest come-ons in the book. He also heard a wealth of emotions—excitement, lust, fear—in her voice. Ones she no doubt thought she had hidden. He needed to get her to some place private, with little chance of interruption, and discover what the hell was going on. Still, a gentleman had to be quite certain of a lady's intentions. "Someplace quiet, preferably alone?"

"Yes."

He rose to his feet and held out a hand. There was no hesitation. He stepped to her side and placed his hand in the middle of her back and guided her from the gardens into the house. To feel the shift of her delicate muscles beneath his hand was both a thrill and torture.

They moved toward the ballroom.

"Are we returning to the ball?"

The avid fascination in her face prompted him to ask, "Would you like to dance?"

She tensed slightly under his touch, then relaxed. "No, of course not," she murmured.

Sweet Christ, how had he forgotten her injury? He glanced down, but she moved with flawless ease. Still, he checked his pace, walking with more care.

Elliot wondered how the hell to deal with her. Remaining incognito seemed important to her. And he was thankful she sought him out and not some stranger. But why had she sought him out? Emma was not the scandalous Fitzgerald. That honor belonged to her sister Maryann, and all she had done to distinguish herself so was eloping to Gretna Green with the local doctor when her family had been against the match.

Emma walked slightly ahead of him almost hurrying, and he knew it was nervous energy. That nervous energy had him on edge. They went up the stairs behind doors leading to the ballroom, and the delicious curve of her rump as she climbed teased him. He should summon a carriage to take her home. But Elliot wouldn't, and he knew in his gut he would come to regret it. Because all he could think about was how much he wanted to run his tongue over the globes of her plump breasts, down to her secret folds, and unravel her one lick at a time. That was how powerful the sway of her hips was.

He gritted his teeth. As soon as he found out what had caused her to flee her country manor, he would send for a carriage. Elliot could not overlook that something had pushed her far enough until she came to him. Not to her brother or even to her best friend, Lady Oliva Newberry. Emma had come to *him*. He tried not to dwell on the savage satisfaction that filled him, and instead prepared to deal with all he saw in her eyes. Lust. Need. And fear.

CHAPTER 4

The pulse and life of the ball swirled inside of Emma, and her heart jerked with both fear and anticipation. She climbed the elegantly curved stairs on legs that wobbled. Nerves fluttered in her stomach, taunting her earlier confidence. She tried to swallow, but her mouth was just too dry. As if Elliot could read her mind, he snatched a glass of champagne from a passing footman and pressed it into her hand.

"Thank you." Her murmur was deep and husky, and Emma realized she did not have to deliberately lower her voice. Fear and arousal were doing a credible job for her. She tried not to feel awkward and out of sorts, moving with careful grace so as not to stumble or cause the damaged muscles in her legs to contract. The very first sight of Elliot in that shadowy corner had filled Emma with shattering awareness, and a heady desire to indulge in something shocking and forbidden with him, and it had not abated. Peeking at him from beneath her lashes, she greedily drank in the well-defined muscles of his arms and shoulders evident through the elegant cut of his dark evening jacket and silver waistcoat. He had that sleek, honed elegance, and if one did not know his background, never would they have imagined that once he had been a little rough around the edges and slightly unrefined.

They reached the landing, and a soft sigh escaped her. It was a relief to know her legs were holding up under the strain of walking without a cane. This was the first she had been able to go this long without rest. Any stumbling now would disrupt the precious moment, and she had crossed the first hurdle to capture his attention. How and why she could hardly care. The doubts had almost crippled her earlier, but now, glimpsing the hot need firing from his eyes eased the nervous flutter in her belly.

Had she captured his regard too easy? Or was he that much of a libertine? A warning hummed inside of her. She caught her bottom lip between her teeth, thinking over the last several minutes. Something had flared across his cheekbones when she'd told him to call her Amelia. Emma felt it was a common enough name and even if he associated it with his best friend's sister, he could not know it was indeed her. He had never seen her without her walking stick or an evident limp, and she had not recognized herself earlier when she'd peered at her transformation in the cheval glass mirror. Certainly, if Elliot knew it was her, he would have called for her carriage and insisted she went home in it.

Please let me be right. This night was too important to her. She had dreamed about every second of the time they would spend together, nothing must spoil this perfect moment. She should have felt awkward. But she didn't.

She felt wild and daring—a lady who knew what she wanted and was about to seize it.

"This way."

She obligingly turned left on the landing, her heels sinking into the thick dark green carpet, bargaining with the butterflies in her stomach. They came to an almost hidden alcove, classical columns and long, red velvet drapes cocooned them into a sort of intimacy. They looked down on the throng, observers of the decadence. Emma was not sure where she got the will from to subdue her anxiety. She concentrated on her desire for Elliot and everything melted away. The glitter of the chandeliers, the dazzling array of dresses the ladies, or not quite ladies, wore, the decadence and laughter. The ornate and exotic masquerade masks. The doubt and the fear, though in truth she was more anxious about the unknown, she was not really afraid of Elliot.

"Sometimes I escape the crush and come here…to watch, to imagine what they are feeling and perhaps to guess as to why they are here, tonight of all nights," he murmured.

She tilted her head and heat speared her as lion-gold eyes ensnared her. Her stomach dipped at the intensity of his stare. A powerful need to touch him seized her, stealing her ability to breathe.

"Are we private enough?"

"Yes."

A multitude of emotions powered through her at that very moment. Doubt, fear, triumph, and relief. She focused on the triumph, and moved closer to him, scandalously close, soaking up the heat of his body. She would doubt no more because the most painful thing that could happen tonight would be to return to her cage without knowing Elliot's touch.

THE FAR EASTERN section of the balcony above the grand ballroom offered some semblance of privacy where they could converse without the temptation of being in a closed room. Though he hadn't attended the house party, he had retained a room, but doors were dangerous. It would be too easy to shut out everything and ravish her. Whenever Elliot had attended Lady Waverly's balls, he'd always retreated to the gardens or the upstairs bowers whenever he wanted a semblance of peace, contented with being away from the throng, the hypocrisy, and the loneliness of being in a sea of people, but not truly connected to anyone.

She stepped to the railing and looked down, eyes scanning the laughing people far below them. "They seem so free," she murmured.

With a sweeping glance, Emma took in the men and women below. She was nervous and was doing her damned best to hide it from him. If he didn't know her, it probably would have slipped right past him.

“That is the point of attending *to be sinful.*”

She had come to him for a reason, and he would not rush her. He tamped down on the need urging him to demand what she was doing there, and why she was dressed with such provocative wickedness. If he scared her and she did something foolish, he would never forgive himself.

A soft laugh tumbled from her throat. “How terribly wicked of the countess to name her house party *Sinful.* I understand it is a weekend of pure extravagance for society to indulge in pleasures and vices. The decadence hinted at in the scandal sheets were not so exaggerated I see,” she said with a glance at a couple embracing intimately by a Corinthian column near the dancers.

He chuckled at the primness that seeped into her voice.

“Do I detect an affront to your sensibilities?”

She laughed lightly, and her shoulders lifted in an inelegant shrug. “Hardly that.”

“Hmm…at least tell me your real name.”

She froze with the glass halfway to her lips, wariness flaring in the depth of her blue gaze. Elliot wondered if he played his hand too soon.

Her lips pursed after a few tense seconds. “Why would you think I’m lying?”

He hesitated, and she stepped boldly toward him, curving her body into his. "And *if* I lied…I assure you it will take more than a demand for me to spill my secrets."

"So, you do have secrets."

"Multitudes of them," her voice was throaty and soft, tempting him. "I give you permission to try to extract them from me."

Was this really Emma? She seemed daring and more alluring than anything he'd ever encountered. How freeing her mask must be to her? If he revealed that he knew her identity would she run from him?

"Why are you truly here?" The need to know burned in his gut.

She took a sip of her champagne, watching him over the rim with a piercing quality that rattled him. He was not a man to be easily rattled.

"For the same reason as everyone. Pleasure."

The "reason" was becoming clear to Elliot, and he fervently prayed he was mistaken in the matter. His cock had stood to attention and had yet to calm down from the way she rasped pleasure. "Are you experienced in erotic liaisons?" he asked wondering how far her ruse extended, and to steer the conversation away from pleasure.

He kept waiting for her to laugh, and say something like "Dear Elliot, how I like to tease you," not that such an absurd explanation would suffice as the reason for this charade because he had ignored her, keeping his careful distance and protecting his heart and pride?

She tilted her glass to her sultry lips, emptying its content before placing the glass on the ledge. She leaned against the balcony railing, brows arched in challenge. "Are you tempted?"

"Yes," he said bluntly.

She gave him a look of drowsy sensuality, and it held him transfixed. Where had she learned to do *that*? She effortlessly pulled him with her innate physicality and pure female seductiveness.

It seemed she wanted to banish Emma completely tonight and immerse herself in however she envisioned Amelia. How irritating it was that she could affect him so easily. Still, he liked her like this. He'd known there was a wicked side to her, deep down. It had seemed like an injustice for someone as beautiful and carefree as Emma to be stifled, to be defined and confined by an accident. How she had pulled away from him and everyone in those first months while she'd been abed. The doctors had declared she would never walk again, and she had proved them wrong. She was resilient and beautiful and brave and unquestionably reckless.

How he had wanted her then, enough to defy his grandmother, the imperious, austere and exacting duchess of Hartford. Elliot had understood why his father had run away to wed his mother and made no effort to claim his connection to the aristocracy. The duchess held no warmth. How she had raged and threatened him when he'd made his intention clear to marry Emma.

Emma, of course, had rejected him. He had asked her for almost two years, and she had kept refusing his offer of courtship until he had stopped asking. Elliot now knew he should have persisted and not have given up on her. Eight years. *Merciful Christ*. It was painful to imagine what they could have been, the joy, the love, the passion they could have had if he had trusted more in the yearning he saw in her eyes.

He considered her, surprised he no longer felt any anger toward her. Though he had burned with fury and pain in those early years, he found little or no emotion had been left inside of him. He had been tired of losing those he loved, and it had been so natural to harden himself against the harshness of heartache. Somehow it had become so natural to him, even the lady he was contemplating to court within the next few weeks hardly inspired anything beyond a gentle appreciation of her genteel beauty.

Emma made him feel.

The only time he'd seen her display some sort of passion was when she played the pianoforte, which she still did in privacy. Now she glowed, the desire for something more gleamed in her gaze, and he wanted to burn with her if only for a fleeting moment.

"You are staring."

Her voice was barely a whisper.

"You are compelling." He cleared the hoarseness from his throat. If he made a mistake and took her in his arms, there would be no denying the heat simmering between them.

She sashayed over to him, slow, sensuous, and he had never known his cock could harden further. He shifted deeper into the shadows, not wanting her to see how easily she affected him. "I've never waltzed," she murmured. "There had been a time I wept with the need to dance just once."

And how could he deny her anything with that heartfelt admission?

She wound her arms around his neck. "Will you waltz with me?"

Her body slid against his in a sexually charged roll, a far too intimate version of the waltz. Emma's hips sashayed in a rhythm that was so beautiful, and provocative Elliot's mouth went dry. A familiar craving awakened inside him, and he wanted to drag her up to his chest and kiss her so badly his teeth ached. He had to resist, for one kiss with her wouldn't be enough.

He spun with her, laid his hands high above her on the wall, eased close so he could speak just beside her ear, ignoring the temptation to nibble. "Why are you here? I am at your disposal if you want to talk." He tried not to come off as too demanding, but damn it, she needed to speak so he could fix whatever the hell made her run away from the safe comfort of her home and into this den of sin. Then he could be out of her tempting presence before he did something stupid.

She leaned against the wall and perused him slowly. "I want you to make love to me…with me."

Her words tore gaping holes through his composure. "I believe I misheard."

"You did not."

He pushed from her, taking a few steps back.

She followed, and the sinuous way she came over to him should have been seductive, but he could see the nerves in her eyes, the slight tremble in her delicate frame.

"I came here tonight for this…for *you*. I want to be made love to by you. I want decadence for the night. Make love to me…Elliot."

CHAPTER 5

Emma's heart was a war drum in her chest. Elliot's hands gripped her hips in a painful vice, but she did not complain. She was too intrigued by the battle flashing across his face. Stark hunger, uncertainty before the coldness won out. She had pierced his armor, and the success of it had all the nervousness fleeing. In fact, she wanted to do a little dance of victory and barely restrained the need.

Instead of pulling her to him, he pushed her away. Though she had spied the raw cravings a few seconds before, his face was a mask of studied indifference. She wouldn't let it disconcert her. Resting her hips on the balcony, she ran her gaze lazily over him. "I'd thought a reputed rake as yourself would have ravished me already."

His brows arched. "Do you now?"

The amusement in his voice piqued her a bit. She wanted him to find her bold and enticing. Nothing else. She shrugged as if his insouciance didn't sting a bit. "Yes. I have heard whispers that called you London's wickedest lover. I've heard that you are truly *sinful.*"

Her voice was a purr in the dark, and Emma kept her eyes glued to his face. Her brother Anthony would roar in rage if he ever discovered how she was shamelessly using an overheard conversation when he had been in his cups to further her own agenda.

Elliot gave her a long, unfathomable glance. "I hesitate to wound you, but you don't want to be anywhere near my wicked desires, princess."

"Don't I?" she sashayed over to him, hoping her walk was provocative and not clumsy. "Why don't you tell me what they are, and I will be the judge of that." She tapped her chin thoughtfully. "Is it spanking?" She had no notion what *that* meant, and Anthony would be truly appalled if he knew she had been in the library trying to sleep that night he had been talking with their cousin, Mr. Thomas Belfry, another rogue of the *ton*.

Surprise flared in Elliot's eyes, then desire.

Emma fought to hold back a sudden smile. "Is that it? It would be such a pity if your wickedness was *only* spanking."

He went still. Yet his was the stillness of a predator stalking his prey. He prowled closer, circling her. She wanted him to kiss her…dear God, she wanted him to kiss her so badly. The last time they had swayed together this close he had kissed her with such longing. It was that night she had fallen so hopelessly in love with him and had never been able to drag herself back to normalcy. *I miss you, Elliot.*

Doing her best to root herself into his moment, she tipped her head back, probing his features in the shadows. "Kiss me."

His lips twitched ever so slightly, and his eyes warmed. "You don't know what you're inviting."

"I do. I want you to make love to me. Tonight."

"Take off the mask," he said, watching her closely.

A sudden rush of fear almost made her jerk from him. This was not part of the script she'd prayed he would follow. "No, the mask stays on… no matter what happens."

The raw flash of pain that seared from his eyes had doubt clawing at her. He stepped back, encasing himself further in the shadows, and she wondered if the bleakness had been her imagination.

A SHAFT of hurt slammed into Elliot's chest, and he ruthlessly buried the telling emotion. Emma wanted him to make love to her, pretending he did not know her identity. Why the hell did that hurt so much?

"Amelia…" he bit back his groan as she twisted and slid her hands around his nape, then thrust her fingers through his hair.

She wanted to walk on the wild side. *With him?* She needed to regain her wits and good senses. Yet the burning desire to succumb to the raging need he'd had for her for years, to draw her into a world of debauched delight ravaged his control.

She pressed her body closer to his, and he could feel every inch of her delectable curves. "I only want tonight, Elliot."

Her voice rang with sincerity, but he could not allow it. His gut burned in denial and cramped in protest. He gripped her hips preventing her from pressing closer. It would not do for her to know how much she had aroused him. "I don't fuck virgins," he said flatly.

She flinched at his crudity, then swallowed.

How he regretted speaking to her in such a manner.

"I'm worldly enough."

He narrowed his gaze taking in her slight blush, and he could see the racing pulse at the base of her neck. His next words were painful to push past his throat, but he could not let her even hope tonight would have the outcome she desired. "I am not a man who is gentle and sweet, princess. You obviously came here tonight for something. That is not with me."

There was a pregnant pause, and then her hands tightened at his nape. "If you do not make love I can f—" she licked her lips. "I can do what you want."

Elliot could not help himself. He laughed. She stiffened, obviously stung at his reaction. Pressing her deeper into the hidden alcove, he dipped his head, his lips perilously close to hers. "You can't even say the word princess, and it is for this reason I am taking you home. You do not know what you are asking. What I want to do to you would scare you, and have you running," he said low and hard, hopefully, mean enough where it would shake her up and encourage her to stop acting recklessly.

Her chin lifted, her lips too damned close, brushing against his. "I will not run."

Yes, you are…to America.

"I must say you will, because I'll debauch every one of your ladylike sensibilities, and I *know* you cannot handle that."

Her voice was breathless, sensual yet questioning, "How?"

He chuckled in disbelief watching her try to process his meaning. Without thinking too deeply about his actions, he inched her gown up to her thighs, his fingers skimming over silken stockings. He was not seductive about it, just matter of fact in his lesson. And he prayed to God she understood this lesson as it was the only way to save them. To save *him*.

Her breath hitched as he nudged her legs wide and cupped her. Elliot froze. *Ah, Sweet Mercy*. She was wet. He battled against the primal urge to drop to one knee, push her legs wider, and taste her. He couldn't believe it was Emma he was touching. *Emma.*

Anthony would kill him.

What scared him the most was that he might give into temptation. And he damn well knew if he made love with Emma there would be no turning back. He would not let her go and would use his considerable influence to ensure she married him, and perhaps he would destroy all that was good and pure in the process. His body throbbed with a relentless ache. She needed to leave, but he couldn't shatter the soft hunger and confidence practically illuminating her with a harsh rejection. The trust she most likely did not realize she stared at him with. If he rejected Emma, she would be devastated, and this confidence, this beautiful daring she radiated would be crushed. That was the last thing he wanted. But if he would send her running, then they would both be safe. It had to be her decision to leave, and the best way to deter Emma, and make her do the rejecting was to allow a piece of his desires to peek out.

He jerked from her and spun her around to face the wall. Even though the alcove was darkened, he did not want to risk her seeing the naked need in his eyes. He gripped her hips and dragged her roughly against him. Elliot wanted her to feel the hard length of his erection pressed tightly against her bottom. He pushed his thigh between hers, lifting Emma to her tiptoes, grinding against the soft, heated pad of her sex.

A tortured groan slipped from him. She was everything he wanted, everything he had dreamed of for ten years. He'd ignored his rising lust every time she flirted with him, ignored the weakness in his gut every time she smiled at him, touched him, and invited him to kiss with her eyes. His fingers itched to stroke over her soft folds and into her silken wetness, and he was starving for the taste of her. He'd kissed her once, and it hadn't been enough. He could kiss her every day, and it would still not be enough. With Emma, he wanted forever.

Concentrate, you moron. This was a lesson meant to send her calling for her carriage and rushing home. He gripped her left hand and wrapped her fingers around the girth of his cock through his trousers. Her delicate fingers had no hope of circling his length fully, and a breath shuddered from her. He hoped her gasp was of trepidation, but a niggling part of him thought it might be arousal. He removed his leg from between hers and stroked his fingers up past her garters and up to her beckoning heat.

She shivered.

He slipped a finger deep inside of her wetness. She was impossibly tight.

"Elliot!"

Her face was a study in pleasure, and he couldn't look away. He had dreamed of this so much, wanting to hear her cries echoing around him as he pleasured her. She arched her back and rested her head on his shoulders, biting her bottom lip as her core contracted around his finger. Blood thundered through his veins, and he closed his eyes, imagining how she would grip his cock.

"I won't lie to you. I hunger to take what you are recklessly offering." And it made him feel like a despoiler of innocents. He groaned at her neck, fighting the need to bend her over and bury his cock deep. "If I cave to my desire, I will take you in ways that will have you running. I will torment you with my tongue and fingers until you are begging for my possession. I wasn't raised as a nobleman, and I do not make love as one."

She gasped, purred and shuddered as he withdrew his finger and pushed back in even deeper. A dull roaring began in his head as wetness bathed his fingers. He struggled to resist. She should be repulsed not excited. He swallowed and prayed that he was successful because his will was fast slipping away. If she did not run, he would take her, and the storm of pain that would unload would be huge. Because once he took Emma, there would be no letting her go.

Run Emma…please sweetheart, run.

CHAPTER 6

Emma's breath strangled in her throat.

Elliot's finger was inside her, and it was without a doubt the strangest and most compelling sensation. It was torture, and it was bliss. And she understood now how many ladies found themselves ruined for pleasure.

She'd always known he would make her feel this way. With just a few words and his wicked caress he brought all sorts of explicit fantasies to the forefront of her mind. She slowly twisted her head and met his eyes. His golden gaze was direct and challenging. He angled his sleek dark head to one side and studied her with unflinching intensity, without a doubt waiting for her reaction to his explicit promise.

"Is that supposed to scare me?"

His chuckle against her ear was low and mocking, yet filled with heated promises. "If I tup you, I will take your mouth first, and I will not be sweet, princess." His tone held a note of warning, and she wondered if he was really trying to scare her away.

He pressed more into her, his erection unmistakable. "Have you ever taken a cock in your mouth?" he growled with sensual menace.

She barely managed to maintain her calm composure. Were such things possible? He was definitely trying to scare her. Trying to make her change her mind. Emma was certain. She wasn't about to, though she felt the heavy press of intimidation. She couldn't even imagine Elliot taking her with the rawness he hinted. Her stomach fluttered with sudden nerves. Emma inhaled deeply. In this, she would not be proper. Not for this one night. She would be bold and adventurous; she would step out of the cage she'd opened fully from the moment she had entered the countess's grand ballroom. "You may ravish me however you want for this night. Let me be wicked with you."

He cursed virulently. She was right. He had not

expected her to acquiesce. All of his crass words were to turn her away.

"Wicked with me?" he drawled menacingly.

"Yes!"

His finger left her body, and she bit back the protest. He trailed fingers wet with her essence up her neck to the corner of her lips. His thumb caressed her lips, and she could smell her own musky scent. She knew he did it to shock her. To show him she would not hide from his passion, she licked his fingers with a slow, deliberate curl of her tongue.

"*Bloody hell.*" His snarl vibrated in her.

He became a statue behind her, and she wished she could see his face.

"I want my sensibilities stripped." Heat crawled up her neck, and she was glad he could not see it. She had already faced a monumental task in seducing him. It would not do for him to see her blushing. "I want excitement, and I want it for tonight. I want your co…cock in me like how you said. Not to be treated like a porcelain statuette of a woman. If you will not do it…"

He became dangerously motionless and her neck prickled in warning, all her instincts screaming for her to tread carefully. "I will not go home this night unsatisfied."

There, that was better than saying she would seek someone else. She prayed he would not call her bluff. Because she wanted no one else, and she would go home cold and empty if he said no. She should have drunk another glass of champagne, at least for more courage. Her stomach quivered, and her knees wobbled. Thank God she hadn't eaten anything, or she would be casting up her accounts and embarrassing herself any moment. She had never felt such nerves before. Not even years ago when she had kissed him and confessed her admiration.

She met his gaze. The intensity of his stare encompassed her entire body. Every dip, every hollow, and every curve felt the caress of his eyes as he probed. Anxiety cramped her gut. What if he knew it was her? Was that why he hesitated?

His voice was rough, deepened with arousal. "Widen your legs."

Emma complied and pressed her face to the wall. The marble tiles cooled her heated cheeks, and she shivered.

"Grip the drapes."

She held onto them. She knew Elliot. He sensed

something about her that made him want to test her reaction. Oh God, what was it? He could not have suspected her. He would have sent her packing already. *Wouldn't he?*

Two fingers suddenly speared inside of her, jerking her to her toes.

Heat, bliss, and a bite of pain cascaded through her core. "Elliot!" It was marvelously wild, and unlike anything she had ever dreamed of. What shocked Emma more than his rough actions was the pleasure that rolled over her, unexpected, seething, and powerful. She quivered, and a low moan, raw and fractured echoed from her lips as wetness gushed his hands.

"For the love of Christ!"

Laughter from below the balcony reached her ears along with the crash of glass. Her pulse fluttered frantically. She knew the alcove was too dark for anyone to see them, but she still couldn't believe the position he had them in. He pressed into her, and she felt every indentation of his body. He kicked her already wide legs even wider and Emma's breathing harshened. His fingers retreated and came back bringing delicious pleasure. He thrust harder, her breath hitched on a whimper, and he froze.

He groaned, and placed a wet kiss on her neck, and then a nip. "You're tight."

"You are talking too much." Her voice was thick with tension, arousal, and her core clenched in hot need.

"Amelia …" The hard body curved around hers trembled.

Emma could practically feel his struggle.

"Look at me," he commanded.

She met his eyes.

"This…the loss of your maidenhead. Do you not want marriage?" His dark golden gaze was direct and curious.

Blood thundered in her ears. "If I wanted a husband I wouldn't be here."

Shadows danced in his eyes before a brief smile touched his lips. "Marriage would bring you a similar pleasure…perhaps more."

Emotions clogged her throat. Tension arced from her to him and uncertainty filled her. "Elliot, I—"

"Turn around," he rasped.

God. She almost revealed herself. Gratefully she obeyed. He placed a finger under her chin and tilted her face toward the soft glow of light, searching her expression. "There is no turning back once we reach my chamber. Do you absolutely want this?"

"I want this…I want *you*."

She grabbed the lapel of his jacket, pulled him to her, rising up on her toes and fastened her mouth to his—hot, wet, hungry, yet so wonderfully tender. *Their first kiss in eight years.* His mouth moved over hers, softly at first, teasing her lips open. Emma was lost in a sea of unending sensation. His lips on hers were everything she'd secretly feared, everything she had ever craved. Exciting. Decadent. Her lips parted, and his tongue plunged into her mouth ravenously.

He shoved her up against the wall, thrusting his hips up into the cradle of her thighs. "Are you sure?"

Heat burned her cheeks, and she hesitated. *This is Elliot,* she reminded herself. *Be honest.* "Yes."

A muscle jumped in his jaw, and his eyes darkened dangerously.

"Why me?"

Emma stared in eyes that glittered with lust and felt such regret she wanted to cry. How she had longed to be with him like this. She wished he knew it was her. She lowered her lashes. "You make me feel so much," she whispered and prayed he did not question it, for her answer was too revealing.

"Look at me."

She glanced up.

Shadows shifted in his eyes. Carnal. Dangerous. "If you stay, I won't let you go home tonight," he promised. "I'll keep my cock buried in you all night long, and I will not hold back with you. There are times I'll destroy your sensibilities where you'll want to run, but I won't let you go."

The breath stilled in her chest, and brutal fists of lust slammed into her stomach. "I know."

He seemed to consider her for a moment, then a slow smile softened the hard edge of his mouth. "I am not sure you understand. I want all of you tonight. *Everything*."

She couldn't stop her shudder. "I want all you have to give as well, Elliot. For tonight."

He gripped her hand and tugged her down the length of the hallway. In silence, he led her toward his guest room. Nervousness and excitement vied for equal attention.

Her heart pounded as they passed several closed doors. Lady Waverley's country home boasted fifty-three rooms, how many would they pass before they reached his? She wanted to sink into Elliot's side, but he held himself rigidly away from her. The silence spoke for them, and it seethed and roiled with hot tension. She glanced at him out of the corner of her eye. She had hardly gotten a chance to really look at him, too caught up in the moment of seducing him. She looked for changes, and somehow, he seemed harder than he'd been a couple years ago. He seemed raw and untamed, all hard muscle yet so beautifully male. His cheekbones seemed sharper, more sensual, and his lips. *God.* They were just as full and perfect, though now they were flattened in a thin line. He stood still with both hands buried in his pockets, but his eyes glittered with sensual intent, promising her everything she wanted tonight. Freedom, wildness, and pleasure. She couldn't handle more. Then she would melt away from his life, treasuring all that he would give her, for one night.

EMMA WALKED SLIGHTLY AHEAD of him. A siren, her hips swaying with a natural temptation that had his cock flexing painfully. He was going to make love to her. He knew with every fiber of his soul, he would not turn her away. Not after craving her for ten years. He did not like the painful knot in his gut, the ache in his chest. It was obvious Emma never intended for their upcoming night to be revealed. He understood why she hid behind the mask, but it still ravaged him to know she would come to him in pretense.

"Here we are," he murmured, twisted the knob, and the door swung open silently.

She swallowed, lifted her chin and swept inside. Dark midnight-blue eyes, nearly black, had seemed overlarge in her pale face. Something inside him clenched at the sight of her obviously pale face beneath the painted mask. Her eyes were wide pools of lust, and was this now apprehension? She was such a contradiction, swallowed up with apparent nerves, then giving him a yearning look, full of innocent desire.

In a bid to give her another chance to leave he spoke, "We can talk, you don't have to—"

She stole the rest of the words from his lips in a bold and aggressive kiss that had his heart jerking. She possessed a wide, soft, voluptuous mouth and she used it to seduce him with tender licks and nips. Amusement curled though him at the thought *he* had to be seduced. His tongue met hers, and they dueled together in a kiss unlike any he'd ever had before.

His hand moved slowly, then his fingers cupping the curve of her cheek, his thumb smoothing over her lips. Elliot knew it to be a grave mistake the second his lips claimed Emma's. He licked slowly across the parted seam of her mouth. Then he kissed her, hard and deep. The taste of her hit his system, hot and intoxicating, making him drunk with need and desire for her.

He was ruined for all other women.

She pulled her lips from his panting. He fought to reason around the lust firing his brain. He wanted her underneath him with a ferocity that appalled him. He glanced at her, probing for fear. Her eyes were large, heavily lashed, still drowsy with arousal, all uncertainty had fled.

He kissed her. She moaned, and he drank in her languid sighs, greedy for more. He kept kissing her as he undressed her. No more talking and no more hesitation. He didn't want to give her any time to change her mind. She'd had enough chances.

He peeled down her gown revealing exquisite breasts, lush and full. He could almost feel them in his hands, in his mouth. He stepped back, running his gaze over her body. A blush ran down her cheeks to her neck and reddened her pale skin. She was gorgeous. His hands inched up her thighs, gently over her tiny waist where the muscles were quivering. Her skin was soft and inviting. Too damn inviting. Dark cravings ate at him even though he'd threatened to ruin her sensibilities he wouldn't. This was Emma. She wanted a night of loving. He couldn't take her with the roughness and the hint of forbidden she had responded to. But God, he wanted to.

"Undress for me," he ordered. Elliot controlled his wince. A part of him was still trying to warn her from him. He waited for her reaction to his command, muscles tense, and his heart jerking too damn fast.

After the slightest of hesitation, and with confidence he'd not realized her capable of, she walked around to the side of the bed. Her movements as she removed her gown were not slow and seductive. They were brisk and to the point. He stepped deeper into the shadows to hide his smile.

"I'll not remove my stockings or my garters," she said huskily, a hint of shadows in her eyes.

And he understood, they would hide the scars.

"As you wish," he murmured, suddenly wishing he could take her in his arms and offer comfort.

She bent in a perfect line, her backside arched to unbuckle delicately heeled red dancing slippers. Those sharp heels against his back would be the perfect edge of pain as he stroked into her. *Stop… this is Emma, I must be tender with her.* His cock throbbed in his trousers, thick and heavy, mocking his determination.

"Leave the shoes."

She paused and glanced up, her eyes probing the shadows for him. She bit her lips, and he watched the expression chase across her face—probably uncertainty because of the commands, then excitement. Her excitement had his cock jerking.

He stripped off all his clothes, his mouth watering to get a taste of her. "Turn around," he whispered. "Remain bent over and widen your legs. I want so see those pretty folds."

She shivered. Then complied. Spinning in a smooth, graceful move. He waited for her to object so he could rein in the needs pumping through his blood like hot liquid.

"Widen your legs more, clasp your ankles, and arch your back," he rasped.

He had to softly clear the hoarseness from his throat as she complied baring her pretty wet folds to his gaze. Would she obey all his commands without question? Was she so bold and brazen that she would ignore her delicate sensibilities, or was this her untapped sexuality, her true nature? He lowered his eyes to the pale, perfect globes of her backside, then lower. From where he stood, Elliot could see the wetness glistening on the folds of her sex, her arousal evident. Stepping from the shadows, he walked over to her, taking in the very provocative pose.

She was perfect.

She trembled as he trailed a finger over the globe of her buttocks down to her cleft. Her skin was like warm satin. “Beautiful,” he murmured, more aroused than he had ever been in his life.

She was so daring, his Emma. So free, and the possibilities had him on edge more than anything else. He ran his fingers down to her wet entrance. She moaned his name as he pushed past the clenching tissue, burying two of his fingers deep in one stroke. She choked his fingers despite her wetness. “You’re so tight you’re killing me, princess.”

“I thought you would approve,” her husky voice taunted.

He chuckled. “I do, very much.”

She sighed and relaxed, even more, the arch of her backside becoming more enticing.

Elliot widened his fingers experimentally and frowned. Her channel was so damn snug he wondered if she would take him comfortably. He didn't want her to hurt tonight unless it was the good kind. "I've never craved a woman as I do now. I want so very badly to work my cock into you…in this very provocative position."

She trembled at the explicit words and actions, her breath panting a little harder. But she did not breathe a word of protest, and lust almost drove him to his knees. Years of bottled need rushed through Elliot, filling him with a depth of craving that scared the hell out of him. She would not run from him or his desires. The surety that he could explore everything with her tonight caused a tremor to course through his body. There would be no ladylike squeamishness despite her innocence. He pressed a tender kiss above the dimple on her ass, then stepped back, fighting for control. "Lay on the bed and spread your legs wide."

Her lips tilted in a small smile, and it was so very arousing. The sensual curve of her mouth was beguiling and so very appealing. She climbed on the bed, lay on her back and extended slender stocking clad legs pressed together high in the air. Then with a slow grace that had his breathing strangling, Emma executed a perfect provocative split baring her pink wet quim to his gaze.

For an endless moment, he couldn't speak, and when he did his voice was hoarse. "Spread them wider. Hold them open if you need to."

She complied, and his breathing deepened. He could not take his eyes off the goddess splayed before him. Her curves were gloriously unbelievable.

Giving in to the gnawing need to taste her, he dipped his head between her splayed legs. She cried out when he licked her slit. She twisted beneath the teasing flicks of his tongue, and his balls tightened as hot fingers of lust stroked up his spine. He sucked her pearl into his mouth. She drew in a harsh breath, then released a moan filled with need. There was no other sound in the chamber, except her soft whimpers and sighs as he licked and nibbled at her wet core. She legs collapsed to rest on his shoulders.

"Oh God, Elliot," she cried out, hips arching into his mouth.

She gripped his hair as he held her open under the lash of his tongue, and pleasured her with decadent greed. When he felt her start to tremble, he drew back and blew softly against her folds, eliciting a fractured moan. He pushed two fingers into her wet heat, twisting lightly, scissoring and widening her snug channel. He slid deftly between her legs and arched her hips to him. He spread her wide, draping her legs over his thighs, so he could look down and watch her take every inch of him. He parted the wet, swollen folds of her sex with his cock and very gently eased into her quivering flesh. His breath hissed from his teeth as he inched in slowly. She was exquisitely tight. She whimpered, closing her eyes as her body stretched to accept his steady penetration.

It was pure ecstasy sinking inside of her. "Look at me, princess I want to see your eyes when I take you." His voice was rough with arousal, and he could feel his control slipping.

Her eyes snapped open, and though they were glazed with pleasure, he saw the discomfort. "Elliot, I…I..."

"We'll go easy," he promised.

Controlling the demands of his body, he slowly slid his cock another inch into her tightness, concentrating on her pleasure. He lowered his head, flicking his tongue across her beaded nipple, then sucking. The tips were hard, dark pink, and felt like satin in his mouth.

She shivered, clenching on his length, and his muscles trembled at the white-hot pleasure that whipped through him. His balls screamed, and he ruthlessly ignored the urge to ride her until they were both raw and sated.

"Kiss me," she whispered with aching need.

He released her nipple and rose up onto his elbow, taking her mouth with a gentleness he had not thought himself capable of at this moment. His tongue swirled, licking in the deep recess of her mouth, savoring her sweetness. His control wavered as she returned his kiss with tender greed. Her fingers twined in his hair as she held him to her, sipping, nipping, and laving his mouth with sometimes playful, then voracious kisses. Elliot eased back and smoothed his thumb over her lips. He dipped his head, claimed her lower lip and bit hard, then soothed it with soft strokes of his tongue. He groaned as she got wetter, more relaxed.

He nudged and slid his cock into her heat another fraction. Her whimper came hard and fast against his lips, her shivers more pronounced, but her sex strained to take him deeper. He wanted to groan her name, pepper praises to her, but he had to reign it in, knowing how devastated she would have been if he made it known he was aware who he held in his arms.

"Take me…just like that. Slow and easy."

Lust was burning inside his gut like acid, and his mutter was more like a growl.

"Not slow…you don't need to treat me gentle. I am not breakable." She rolled her hips underneath him, a move that was so sensuous and scorching, sweat beaded on his skin.

She pressed her lips against his ear, her voice one of carnal temptation. "Take me, Elliot…*ruin* me."

He pushed forward, forcing her to take half his length and girth in a hard thrust. A wild cry tore from her throat. She trembled, her wet heat swallowed him, and wrapped him in sublime tightness and soothing comfort. He had never been this damned hard for a woman in his life, and he was determined to kill her with pleasure, so she would be unable to walk away.

Not from this.

Not from him and the possibilities.

He did not care what he had to do to ensure their future, but secure it he would. *You are mine, Emma Amelia Fitzgerald.*

CHAPTER 7

Emma rode an edge of pleasure so sharp and consuming it terrified her. Impaled on Elliot's hardness, she moaned helplessly at the fullness of his penetration. Each slow plunge which urged her to take his thick length ignited a burst of fire deep down in her stomach, but she could still feel the restraint in his touch, see it in his gaze. Knowledge suddenly welled from the depth of her beings. "Help me chase away the loneliness," she whispered, lifting her legs to wrap around his hips, the silk of her stockings gliding smoothly over his back, the edge of her slippers pressing against his skin. "*Ruin* me, my darling." Her own voice sounded strange to her.

The savage hunger that moved in his eyes and

tightened the skin over his cheek bones should have scared her. But it enthralled her. He withdrew, and he returned to the depth of her body with a swift and deep penetration, filling her with pleasure and pain. Her eyes fluttered close as she absorbed the shocking impact of his thrusts on her senses.

"Don't look away from me," he groaned.

Her lashes lifted, their gazes locked. She could get lost in his eyes. They glittered with lust and tenderness. The tenderness confused her for it hinted at familiarity, but before she could even start to think, he ground into her with deep, powerful strokes, and she lost herself in the dominant eroticism of being taken by him.

She gasped as he splayed her more open and thrust even deeper. The sensation of being stretched so widely was erotic. Moans and whimpers she could not prevent ripped from deep inside as she pleaded for Elliot to never stop. He arched her, dipped his head, and raked his teeth over the sensitive tip of her nipple.

"Can you take more?" he whispered, his tone rougher than before. "Can you take me harder, deeper?"

Her body responded violently and instinctively to the explicit promise of more. "Yes," she gasped.

"Sweet gorgeous woman," he growled.

His hips snapped harder in an unrelenting rhythm, and she sobbed, dimly aware of the hoarse cries spilling from her throat. She gripped the sheet in her fists, as the sharp edge of pleasure-pain he invited her to ride with each thrust became unbearable. Sensations gathered in her stomach, sending uncontrollable tremors through her thighs, and before her mind could process it, delightful pleasure arched through her more intense than anything she'd ever felt. Relentless waves of pleasure engulfed her entire body, and Emma came apart with a loud unexpected cry of relief.

Three strokes later, Elliot crushed her to his chest and with a rasping groan released inside of her. He kissed her lips with a gentleness that had her heart aching. He stroked her hair, a tender gesture that made her sigh, then dropped his forehead to hers, his breathing ragged, staring into her eyes for what seemed like endless seconds. She so badly wanted to say 'Elliot, it's Emma.'

"Are you well?"

Her throat closed, and she nodded. The need for him to know that it was her had a knot of emotions choking her. Before she could do something foolish, he pulled from her and slowly withdrew his member. Her breath caught at the slight discomfort. He pushed from the bed, the flickering fire cast dancing shadows over his naked form. Elliot was so beautiful, his muscles hard and powerful.

Even in the low light, the red blush that flushed her entire body as he took a cloth or perhaps his handkerchief and cleaned between her legs were evident. Whatever he had used was discarded on the pile of clothes scattered on the carpeted floor.

Elliot watched her, his gaze hooded, face set in stark, sensual lines. "Are you sore?"

She was, but Emma felt mesmerized by the carnal promise glowing from his eyes. "Why?"

She gasped silently at the amusement that tugged at the corner of his mouth. There was a promise of wicked delights in that half smile. And God, she wanted to rise on her knees and lick the smile away, then continue down to the rippling walls of his chest and abdomen. Who knew she was the possessor of such wanton urgings.

Golden eyes rested possessively on her face. "Weren't you warned about what I would want from you, princess? That you would be on my cock all night long?" He answered with a drawl that had a shiver working up her spine.

Heat curled low in the pit of her stomach, jolting her. "You did," she said softly. She rose to her knees and sat on her haunches, watching him.

He tugged her to him, taking her lips in the softest and sweetest kiss she had ever received. "If you want me to stop, I will. Just say the words. We can go dancing. We can do anything you want."

She clasped his neck pulling him to her, taking his lips into a deeper kiss. "I want everything you have to give. Tonight. No regrets."

The slightly crooked smile he gave caused a deep flutter in her belly. "No regrets," he murmured, smoothing his hands over her hips and down to her stocking clad legs. Her heart lurched, and she hoped he would not ask her to remove them. He lowered himself and removed the dancing slippers from her feet. He stood, rocked back on his heels, gazing down at her with a mixture of hunger and amusement that made her shiver.

With firm but gentle hands, he turned her, so she lay on her stomach. She was acutely aware of his gaze on the hollow of her spine, the curve of her buttocks.

He came over her like a warm, sensual blanket, coasting his hand over her buttocks and down to her sex. His finger probed, he grunted his approval, and she blushed.

She was already shamelessly wet for him.

He slid his hands around her hips to her derriere, then lifted her up onto her knees. Soft but firm kisses were pressed on her shoulders and down the curve of her spine.

Her body was wet, soft, and yielding, accepting the hard length that surged deep inside, but even so, her muscles quivered to accommodate his thickness. She needed to breathe, to scream out in pleasure, but she could only whimper into the sheets at the soul searing bliss. How long he made love to her, she couldn't possibly have known. He never stopped moving, never stopped touching her. It seemed like forever. If only she wasn't damaged, this could indeed be forever.

What felt like hours later, Emma lay onto her side, the sheets covering her body, feeling exhausted but wonderful. Sounds of Elliot's feet padding away reached her ear, then the sounds of servants filling the bath from behind the screen. Seconds later, the bed dipped, and strong arms curved under her back and knees, lifting her. It felt wholly natural to rest her head against his chest and snuggled into him.

"Are you well?" His voice was soft, concerned. "I fear I may have been too enthusiastic."

And now she was delightfully tender, and she blushed at the awareness. "Are you well?"

She felt his smile against her hair.

"You were better than anything I could have imagined."

Tears burned beneath her lids, and she wanted to scream. She had hungered for years to hear such words from him, and now he said them not knowing it was her. He entered the bathroom and lowered her gently to her feet. She blushed as he took a warm wash cloth and cleaned between her tender folds and around to her bottom. With such care, she felt no discomfort, only a sense of awe.

Was he this way with all his lovers?

She pushed the thought of him pleasing other women from her mind. Tonight, was for her, she would not let her insecurities intrude. He placed the washcloth on the basin's surface and drew her to him. He cupped her cheeks and teased at the eye mask. Questions formed in his golden gaze, ones she was afraid to hear. "I will not remove it," she said softly before he could ask.

His eyes dipped to her stockings and garter.

"Nor them," she said softly.

"They will get wet."

"It does not signify." She could not bear for him to see the scars on her legs. Not only would he know her identity right away, he had never seen that ugly mess of tissue before. What if he were to react with disgust? Or pity? Either would rip through her heart.

A cynical smile shaped his lips, and she fought the urge to rip the mask off her face and scrub the paint away. Pulling from their embrace, he tested the water, then stepped in. He held out his hand to her, and Emma did not hesitate. They sank into the depth of the tub, and she moaned in delight as the hot water seeped into her muscles, soothing places she had not realized were sore.

"Thought you would like it." He pressed a kiss to her nape.

She relaxed fully into his sculpted chest, thankful he was not broaching the topic of her need for anonymity. "Tonight has been incredible, I will treasure the memory."

He buried his face in her hair, and her heart jolted.

"You speak as if the night is over. Is it your habit to forget promises?"

I'll keep my cock buried in you all night long, and I will not hold back with you.

Not over as she'd thought.

Just the beginning.

EMMA AWOKE SILENTLY. The heat of the body curved behind her made her realize the graphic images blaring through her mind had not been a dream. She had made love with Elliot, over and over before sliding into an exhausted slumber. She listened to the rise and fall of his chest and determined by his steady breathing that he slept. She twisted gently to face him, bracing herself for the impact. It rose in a sweet, gentle swell, sensations she hardly knew what to do with. She smiled, unsure of what she expected. He seemed so fierce and raw when awake…now he looked at peace. Her smile grew wider. She had given him that. Peace, and without a doubt, mind blowing pleasure. Heat crawled up her face as she remembered the praises he had whispered to her, hot explicit praises and promises as he took her for the night.

This is goodbye, Elliot. A few weeks from now she would be on a ship to America.

Raw, visceral emotions tore through her, grief scalded the back of her throat, and her senses reeled. She burned to wake him and kiss him, just once more, though she suspected no matter what she experienced with Elliot, it would never be enough. She gingerly eased from the bed, wincing at how her body ached. Emma gathered her clothes and went behind the dressing frame. Her legs ached, and she desperately wanted a warm compress. She took a steadying breath and dressed without the aid of a maid. Perhaps she could ring for assistance, but that would certainly wake Elliot.

From time to time she paused to peek around the frame to ensure his breathing remained steady. She wondered what to do. Did she leave him a note thanking him for the incredible night? What would he do when he woke and found her gone? Would he wonder who she was and want to see her again? Emma shook the fancy away. Not once for the long night had he mentioned anything that suggested he would want to know more about her. Clearly, he was used to liaisons such as these, and it was foolish for her throat to burn so. But she could not help feeling a little deflated that he had not known it was her. That he had been so wild, raw, and intimate with a stranger.

She slipped out of the bedroom and down the empty hallway silently. She had left explicit instructions for the carriage to be ready by five this morning. Thankfully she hadn't overslept. The sound of light revelry reached her ears, and she paused. The ball was not yet over. Moving gingerly, she started to descend the stairs, ensuring she used the railings for assistance. She swiped at her tears. She was terribly foolish for crying. But it felt like her soul hurt. Being with Elliot was probably a bloody mistake. She grimaced. It felt good to curse. It was breaking her heart to walk away. It physically hurt. To know that she could only have this one night. It would have been better if she'd never known what it could be like in his arms.

A dark shadow climbed the stairs, and it was as the person faltered, she glanced up. Emma froze. Anthony. *Oh, God.*

Perhaps he would not recognize her in her wig and dress. But perhaps she should not risk passing him so closely. She turned around and started to make her way back up the stairs. Where she would go, she had no notion, for the chamber with the sleeping duke was not an option. Her brother was clearly a guest and would have a chamber. She would wait until he entered his assigned room and then turn back. Perhaps she moved too fast, for her leg knotted, and she slapped her hand over her mouth to muffle the cry of pain. She bent, and knead the muscles of her calf, deeply, working out that tight knot of anguish. The pain eased, and she breathed a soft sigh. Profound relief swept through her that it hadn't turned into an episode.

"Emma?"

His shocked tone arrested her retreat. *Dear God, how had he recognized me?*

She straightened and slowly turned.

"What are you doing *here*?"

She could think of no possible reply. Her brother wiped his hand over his face slowly, shook his head, and stared at her unblinking. Dark blue eyes so like hers shifted up to the hallway behind her, and his gaze remained there for long, silent moments. Why was he at Lady Waverly's country manor. She and Maryann had asked him on separate occasions, and he had said he would be in town. Her heart pounded as she watched Anthony's face while he processed the fact that his sister had obviously just come from one of those chambers, and it did not require a genius to deduce which one.

This man was her older brother, one of her only safe anchors in her world, and she hated the pain that chased across his features. Even if it was unwarranted.

"Anthony, I—"

He slashed his hands, and her words tapered off. His gaze swung back to her, no doubt taking in her tear-stained face, her mussed hair, her swollen lips, the love bites trailing from the globe of her breasts toward her neck, and her scandalous red dress. Something vicious moved across his face, and she flinched.

"Did you tell him no?" he asked gently even though she could see the dark anger in his eyes.

She jerked. Was he asking her if Elliot took advantage? *"I beg your pardon?"*

"Did you *try* to tell him no, Emma? Did he seduce you?" Anthony demanded with lethal softness. Save the furious working of his jaw, he was still as he stared at her.

Her throat tightened. "What are you asking me, Anthony? Elliot is your friend, are you really asking me if he forced his attentions on me?" She could hardly credit her brother was wondering such a ghastly thing.

Something violent moved in his gaze. "Answer the *bloody* question, Emma."

She stepped down a few steps, angrier than she'd ever been toward him. "I will not just answer your *bloody* question," she snarled.

He raised his brow at her curse words, but she powered ahead. "How dare you insinuate Elliot would do something so disgusting?"

"I did not mean it like that," he growled.

"Then what did you mean it as?" she demanded, incensed.

"Devil take it, I know his reputation is not rumors. We're friends."

"Then act like his friend. Elliot has honor."

Anthony's broad shoulders relaxed, barely. "Then why the hell are you crying? Why do you look so…wrecked?"

He hurried to her side, took her hand and assisted her down the final steps. "Emma?"

She gave him a withering look. "You do not get to ask me that after what you implied about Elliot," she said, her voice breaking as more tears gushed forth.

Anthony had the grace to look discomfited. He raked his hand through his hair and sighed. "I'm sorry. I lost my head for a few seconds when I saw you. Your lips were swollen. And your eyes, Emma… they were…" he grimaced. "I have never seen you dressed in such a fashion. You shocked me."

She nodded. "Apology accepted."

They made their way down the hallway, and she noted her brother looking around to ensure they were alone.

"Why are you crying?"

He was so tenacious. She couldn't prevent the blush that heated her entire body and met his eyes. "Because I am in love with him, and I know nothing will come of feeling the way I do." She knew these were not things one admitted to your brother, but they had always been close, and he was prying. And she was no longer a child.

He predictably stiffened. "Damn it, Emma. We will talk about this at home. But you seem to have mistaken the matter."

"There is nothing to talk about, Anthony. I chose to attend this masquerade ball for my own purposes, I was not coerced or ruthlessly seduced by some libertine as you no doubt imagine. I suspect you've always known how I feel about Elliot, so please don't make a fuss out of me being here. You are the one who is mistaken in the matter."

"He will marry you," he said softly.

She closed her eyes, trying to breathe evenly. "No, he will not."

"I will make him. I do not care if he is the goddamned duke of Hartford and that he is reputed—"

"I'll not have him," she whispered furiously. She knew she could not have him. Any pity or remonstrances from Elliot would wound her soul. "This was not some elaborate plan to compromise Elliot into marriage, and you will not make it be about that. I'll be leaving soon, and I'll not be forced to stay."

Her brother said something rather obscene and unflattering under his breath. Her coat was collected, and she deftly slipped it on with his help. "You were never supposed to discover I had been here. No one else knows, and we will keep it that way."

At his silence she gripped his hand, rushing to speak as the butler opened the door and they spilled out into the chilling dawn. "Elliot doesn't even know it's me." She pointed to her painted face that had not even washed away with how she'd sweated.

"What you have done is beyond disastrous, Emma."

She sighed. "You are just trying to scare me when there is no need."

Her carriage was waiting as expected and they moved toward it. Emma walked at a brisk pace, conscious of the pain in her leg, grateful the place seemed so isolated.

Anthony expelled a frustrated breath, keeping pace beside her. "There will be dire consequences, and it is my duty and honor to protect you," he said firmly with an admirable show of brotherly concern.

"There is nothing to protect me from. I was not taken advantage of. And most importantly, His Grace has no notion…no notion it was me in his chambers."

He didn't seem to appreciate the reminder that she had been so wildly improper from the snarl that curled his lips.

Before he could snap, she hurried on, "And it is my wish for my identity to be hidden from the duke, and I will have your loyalty, Anthony," she insisted once again, pointing to the painted mask.

He grunted and gave her a look of incredulous disbelief. "He knew it was you, Emma. Elliot knew it was you."

Apprehension jolted through her. "No, he did

not. Elliot hasn't called upon me in a very long time. He was only a fleeting presence at the manor last week. The only reason you recognized me was that you saw me *yesterday* and because I had a slight episode. Please leave it be, Anthony. Promise me you won't say anything. I don't want anyone involved in my private affairs least of all you." She smiled to take the sting out of her words.

Anthony held her gaze. "This was only one night?"

"Yes, I promise."

They reached the carriage, and he assisted her in. He entered and sat opposite her, leaning against the squab. His gaze raked her figure several times, and the shock that had flared in his blue depths each time made her blush.

"At least you had the presence of mind to disguise yourself and the carriage."

"There is no need to escort me, you may continue as you will."

"I am taking you to Bellview manor." His hard tone brooked no arguments. She nodded in acquiescence, knowing the need roiling inside of him demanded that he saw her safely home.

The carriage pulled away, and with a sigh, she relaxed her shoulders. A few minutes passed in silence before profound irritation snapped through her. "You are staring, Anthony!"

His gaze narrowed. "You don't understand how it unsettles me to think of you alone with the duke for even an hour."

Fire licked her body at his blunt statement. She had been with Elliot for hours, and she shifted her eyes from his, lest he read the knowledge there. She didn't think she'd been fast enough.

"*The Goddamned bastard*."

"Please refrain from being crude," she snapped.

"Emma, I know the duke's exploits and conquests, if he had not known it was you he would have had no reason to be protective of your delicacy. I doubt you can speak to me right now about being crude. And we will stop talking about this before I break my promise and challenge him for taking your honor."

Tears sprang to her eyes, and she nodded in quick agreement, fighting the mortification and fear that tried to engulf her. She prayed she had not caused a rift in their friendship. "Please do not speak so lightly of dueling, Anthony. Elliot has been your friend for years."

"Then you shouldn't have acted with such recklessness," her brother snarled.

Unable to speak anymore, so intense were the emotions tearing through her, Emma closed her eyes, hating that the tears spilled over.

Her brother sighed and said her name with soft regret, but she ignored him, closed her eyes, and remarkably a smile tipped her lips.

She had been brave and free and improper. And for now, that was all that mattered.

CHAPTER 8

Emma turned her iron key into the lock and slipped quietly into the manor, thankful the household still slept. She'd convinced Anthony he needn't escort her inside. He'd still shimmered with fury, but it had lessened on the drive over. The control he'd exerted over his emotions had been visible, and commendable. She had long accepted that even when she was sixty, Anthony would see her as his to protect. But she would have no further discussion on her one night of passion.

She'd encouraged him to return to the house party, after securing his promise he would not betray her confidence. Hurrying up the stairs, she made her way to her chamber and opened the door. Calm stole over her the minute she stepped into her bedchamber. Warm and inviting, designed in shades of light green, her room reflected what she liked, and not what was fashionable amongst the elites. The most wonderful thing about her room was that one side was lined with long, rectangular windows which were edged with brightly colored stained-glass. There she would sit for days and overlook the beauty of the land, whether it be bedecked with flowers in bloom or the haunting snowy white of winter. If she looked away from the windows, she could imagine it was spring or a glorious summer day, and she was in a lush garden surrounded by dense verdure. She could picture herself in foreign lands with jungles closing in on her. The sounds of exotic birds and the chatter of agile monkey had filled her daydreams. There would be no jungles in America, no mischievous monkeys, but there would be an adventure. She would experience new things and meet new people. From that window, she watched the garden parties her mother hosted, the picnics with neighbors, and there she sat and painted, and dreamed, and often remember all the glorious times with Elliot. There would be no Elliot in America, she thought before her reverie was broken.

"Where have you been?"

She faltered at the sharp question. Her gaze swung to the figure seated in the dark on the blue chaise against the left wall near her windows. "Upon my word, Aunt Beatrice, what are you doing here?"

Aunt Beatrice, really Lady Covington after having her own whirling and scandalous courtship with a viscount, surged to her feet and glared at her. "Why are you dressed in such a positively scandalous manner?"

The outraged question started a pounding inside of Emma's head. The irony was that her red satin dress was less revealing and provocative that many dresses her sister and mother had worn to balls. But Emma's life had been so conservative, so dull, a barely-there décolletage was enough to induce shock. "I was at a ball," she said softly.

"I beg your pardon?"

Emma inhaled deep and drew from her well of patience, the one she had always used to deal with her family since her accident. "Is there a reason you are in my chamber, aunt?"

"Why are you in masquerade?"

Impatience bit her. "Aunt Beatrice, why are you here?"

"Why will you not answer my question? Which

ball did you attend and why was I not informed of this?"

She steeled her spine, ignoring the shaft of pain that arrowed through her legs. "It isn't important why I'm dressed how I am, or where I've been. That is my concern only." She tried to sound firm but feared the defensive posture of her hands clasping her middle gave her away.

Her Aunt blanched. "I must summon your parents from Bath at once."

The pounding behind her temple worsened, and she stepped past her Aunt and lowered herself onto the edge of her bed. A soft groan of relief escaped her. She would need a hot bath immediately to sooth the tension insidiously working through her muscles, and then she would need to rest for the remainder of the day.

"Were you in town? Which ball are you coming from?"

Her aunt would harangue Emma until she got an answer that confirmed her worst suspicions. "I was at Lady Waverly's masquerade ball." There. She admitted it.

Aunt Beatrice scanned Emma's body with new knowledge. Her lips pinched, fire spat from her eyes, and fury tautened her frame. "How could you so wantonly ruin your prospects with Lord Coventry? *Why* would you go there, of all places?"

Emma rubbed her temple. "You still have not informed me why you are in my chambers."

Aunt Beatrice advanced, her strides militant. "Did anyone recognize, you? Dear God, was your limp evident? I demand to know why you were at such a sordid affair and with whom?"

The scathing question had Emma's stomach churning. Pain seared her heart, and long held insecurities tried to swamp her.

The night had been perfect for her, and anger surged that she'd allowed her aunt to rouse her fears so easily, and with such few words. Emma did not need this. Nothing was going according to plan. Her one night was supposed to be her treasured secret. "I will not discuss this with you, Aunt Beatrice. Not now. In fact, not ever. I am five and twenty, and what I do in my private life is just that. *Private.*"

"My goodness, how can you be so uncontrite? Lord Coventry —"

"Please stop, Aunt Beatrice." Emma tugged the wig from her hair, unpinned her hair, and raked her hand through her tumbled mess of hair, painfully conscious of the tender burn between her legs. The mask on her face was also starting to itch. "I am exhausted, and I need a bath if you would excuse me."

She ignored the scandalized look her Aunt sent her way.

"Please see yourself out of my chambers."

"I will not leave until I receive an explanation from you, young lady," Aunt Beatrice charged.

Her heart clamored, but she forced the words past her lips. "I owe you no explanation of my actions."

"Your life is not your own. How dare you think so?"

Rage, hot and wicked, flared inside of Emma. She had never heard her put it so bluntly. Her life was not her own? "It isn't, is it?" She briefly closed her eyes. "I doubt you will be able to understand this, Aunt Beatrice, but I implore you to try. It was, for this reason, I went to Lady Waverly's ball. I wanted something for *me*. I have done everything you, Anthony, mamma, and papa have encouraged me to do, from ever since I can remember. So, allow me this one night without making a hash out of it, please. There was no ruin or scandal or anything terrible that will be revealed."

She stood and brushed past her aunt, who stood

frozen in some sort of stunned silence and rang the bell pull for a maid to attend her. Emma hurt so damn much.

Her aunt quietly departed, and Emma closed her eyes tightly for a few seconds fighting back the tears. She was glad Aunt Beatrice had not decided to stay and fight. Her eyes had been huge pools of shock and betrayal. But Emma could not help that. She'd not expected anyone to discover her wild night. Now Anthony and her aunt knew, and Emma did not delude herself for one moment that her father and mother would not soon be the recipient of her aunt's lurid imagination. They would travel from Bath with all haste, and try to stifle her with their love and fears.

Emma would never apologize for an experience that was so intensely personal and wonderful. She had her one night. No more dancing too close to the fire. But her mother wouldn't be able to understand that.

A maid bustled in, and Emma ordered a bath to be delivered to her chamber. She slowly undressed, peeling the stockings from her legs, observing how red and chafed her skin appeared. There were deep scars that ran from her shin, up to her thighs, hideous gouges in her flesh. Her bone had been broken and re-cast three times in those early months, and the fight to stave off infection had been brutal. She hated recalling to her mind the feel of the wind on her face as the curricle had raced across the lanes, Anthony's frantic pull on the reins of the horses, and her brother's hoarse cry of fear as they'd tumbled over. Closing her eyes against the memories, she reclined on the bed as the servants bustled in with pails of hot water, filling the copper tub behind the screen.

"Miss Emma, the bath is ready for you."

With a soft sigh, she pushed from the bed, and removed the last of her clothes with the maid's assistance, noting the maid's careful manner in not looking at her mangled legs. Emma stepped into the bath, and slowly sat in the large tub, the water sloshing gently over the side. The hot lavender scented water washed over her, relaxing her muscles. She lathered her face with her special blend of soap and gently scrubbed the paint away.

Elliot had been so wonderful. *So, everything*. He'd been the perfect mixture of domination and tenderness. Hours later she still retained the sensation of him making love with her, still could feel the hard imprint of his body against her back, the phantom caress of his manhood shuttling in and out of her. It had been erotic just to watch the pleasure she'd given him. And he had not known it was her. The sob was dredged from the pit of her soul, and the tears came freely. She knew it was best he did not know it was her, but it hurt terribly.

She'd wanted him forever. Emma had never really understood the nature of romantic attachments until she started dreaming of him being her first in everything. He had been there for her for years. Comforting her aches, the ones Anthony hadn't been able to soothe, and featuring in all her girlish fantasies of knights and honorable heroes. He'd been the one to teach her how to make a proper fist, how to swim, and how to fish. All unladylike endeavors and he hadn't berated her for having the desires. He'd been her first and only kiss. *And he'd not recognized anything about me?*

Emma stiffened as knowledge teased her subconscious. *He'd called me princess.* How had she not noticed? Rinsing her hair and body quickly, she stepped from the bath, deep panic winding through her heart. Elliot had referred to her as princess several times. As he had *always* referred to her. Her guard had been so lowered by the sheer enormity of her ruse she hadn't noticed.

Emma felt breathless and slightly ill.

Drawing on her robe, uncaring her skin was still wet, she thought at a rapid pace. *Perhaps I am overreacting.* The duke could possibly call every woman princess. Surely if he had known it was her, he would have turned her away.

Wouldn't he?

CHAPTER 9

Emma was gone.

Elliot had felt her slipping from the bed and had ruthlessly prevented himself from halting her. She'd only wanted one night of scandalous passion. He tried to leave it at that. God, he wanted to leave it at that. But he couldn't. He'd desired her for far too long. He had always dreamed of her, and it had scared the hell out of him. He'd woken from blistering hot dreams, which had changed to sweet and endearing. He didn't just want her body, he wanted everything. Her smiles, laughter, pain, love. *Everything*.

Elliot had let her go then. She had been too young, and he had been too damn uncertain, hesitant of denting her surety of not wanting to marry. He was tired of hiding what he felt for her, just plain tired of being alone, tired of being so damned unresolved where she was concerned.

He did not know what precipitated her actions last night, but she'd finally come to him. Emma was a woman that craved a life she did not know how to embrace. A life she would only indulge in behind a mask. And Elliot was going to peel back the layers for her. Strip her bare and reveal the woman of passion and boldness he had met last night.

How she had taken him for the night. With hot sweet hunger. Definitely not a girl anymore, but a woman of daring passions. He'd seen the loneliness in her eyes when she talked about wanting more. He could hardly tolerate the people he mingled with daily for business or even those in the *ton*, but at least when he went to his country seat, he had deep soul peace. Emma didn't have that. When the chips had been stacked against her, the walls pressing in on her, she'd turned to him. That meant something, and he wanted to explore that. Elliot was sure her family would welcome his courting of Emma, but he wasn't sure if she would.

He pushed from the bed and with practice ease, he dressed. For so long he had done without a valet, on most days he was still able to present a respectable picture without aid. Several minutes later, Elliot was riding his horse along the lanes of the countryside heading to his home in Kent. It made no sense to stay for the remainder of the house party, it had lost its allure. Now he needed to plan his campaign of how he would seduce Emma. She might even now be with child. *Sweet Mercy*. The pleasure that tore through him at the very image of her swollen with child. A rider approached, riding as if the devil were on his heels. Elliot frowned and slowed his mount as he recognized Anthony. What was he doing heading towards the countess's property? Had something happened to Emma?

Anthony came to a shuddering halt and swept off his steed. Elliot dismounted his gut tightening. "Is it Emma? Is she well?"

"You dishonored my sister."

He jerked to a stop at the words that barreled from Anthony's mouth. Elliot stiffened. Anthony's face was blank, his face carefully neutral, except for his eyes. They blazed with anger and knowledge. Too much anger. And it gutted Elliot to see it. Eight years ago had been the last time Anthony had warned him away, and he was still doing it. Except then he hadn't been a Duke, but he was still not good enough in his best friend's eyes. Elliot never thought it would hurt. But the feelings twisting in his gut was more than disappointment. "You don't know what happened between us, Anthony."

"Really? Emma looked thoroughly ravished to me," he snarled, fisting his hands at his side. "You couldn't have said no? She swished her scantily dressed body in front of you, and you lost your fucking mind?"

Elliot slammed his fist into Anthony's mouth without hesitation, dropping him on his ass. Anthony was calm as he swiped the small speck of blood from the corner of his mouth with his thumb. The man was like a brother to Elliot, but the raw violence that shimmered in his eyes, which were just like Emma's, lacked brotherly affections.

Elliot held out his hand, and Anthony clasped his forearm as Elliot helped him to his feet. This was not how Elliot wanted the revelation of his and Emma's relationship to come to light. Anthony was not a man to be trifled with. But it was more than that. Elliot did not want to hurt him. "Call me all the names you want. I will give you the fight you want, and we can pound the hell out of each here, at my home, or even at Gentleman Jackson. But don't you ever speak ill of Emma," he said sounding far calmer than he felt.

"I promise I will hurt you if you do, friendship or not."

"I deserved that," Anthony admitted, then a cold smile curved his lips. "Let's go now."

He shook off his jacket and unbuttoned his shirt, shrugging out of it, and tossing his clothes on the grass, and Elliot cursed mentally.

Elliot smiled, accepting the cold burn of anger that pulsed through him. They hadn't fought down and dirty in years. It had always been with correct form and perfect execution when they sparred. Elliot chuckled as he heard the cracking of knuckles behind him. It was about to get messy. And there was no way around it. He accepted that. There had always been an unstated code between them, sisters were off limits to ravishment. It would be Anthony's right to issue a challenge or thrash him within an inch of his life.

Elliot shrugged from his superfine jacket and faced Anthony. The man was muscled, definitely more so than Elliot. But he knew he was faster, more vicious, and dirtier. Not that he wanted to fight to win, but Anthony would fight even harder if he thought Elliot was taking it easy.

He rolled back his shoulders, meeting the icy calm in Anthony's gaze.

"You should have turned her away," he said. "I know you recognized her."

"I did."

Anthony's eyes narrowed to dangerous slits. "I demand satisfaction, and you will marry her, or by God, I will call you out."

Elliot needed to own his intention. The only person he would really worry about rebelling against his claim would be Emma. But he knew with everything in him she was strong enough, and she only needed to recognize it herself. She had an inner core of strength that she hid from the world. He had spied it over the years, and last night she had burned him with that wild, strong, beautiful vixen inside of her. She did not shy from his dominant nature, and he needed a duchess, a wife, a friend, who would never be afraid to defy him, to push back when needed. And that woman was Emma, and only her, she was a dove but also a lioness. Damn if he would hide it anymore. "I'm going to marry her."

"You should have married her, and then, and only then, take what she must have foolishly offered. For honor and friendship sake, you should have found the willpower."

Anthony's fist snapped out, and Elliot's head

slammed back from the force of the blow. *Bloody hell.* He rolled with it, and when Anthony came under his flank, Elliot was prepared. They dipped and weaved, grappled with each other, and more than once got down hard and rough in the grass. Elliot was not sure how long they fought. But he lost himself in the moment, in the sheer beauty of fighting; trading blows that damn well hurt.

"Are we done?" he snarled to Anthony, gingerly feeling along his ribcage. It would be tender for at least twenty-four hours.

Anthony wiped at the blood that trickled from his nose, eyes narrowed and chest heaving. Elliot saw the knowledge in Anthony's eyes that they were evenly matched. They had both been taking it easy with each other. Friendship and all. Though Elliot could feel the bonds of that friendship straining and trembling, and he prayed it did not break.

"She will not marry you, despite her being ruined. I would be a poor friend to allow you to hope in vain." Anthony sounded truly sincere.

"I mean to persuade her," replied Elliot. And it was an unpleasant thought, offering up his heart once more to a lady who truly did not seem interested in it. He realized that the dart of apprehension which was arrowing through him was decidedly unpleasant. But he would not run from it, the chance to be with her forever would be worth it.

Anthony scrubbed a hand over his face. "To do something this stupid and reckless proves how much she wants you. However, you will not succeed in persuading her heart to marriage. We've thrown four suitors at her overs the years, all of good family, with wealth and connections. She's rejected them all. Now she is of age with her own money, I truly fear she means to travel to America and away from father's constant pressure to use her to elevate our family further."

Elliot stumbled toward the large oak tree and leaned against its massive trunk, hating to remember her certainty of one night.

"What will you do?"

Elliot schooled his face and glanced at his friend. He felt gutted, but Anthony didn't need to see it. "I will approach your father and make an offer."

Emma belonged to him. And he would prove it. Not to Anthony or her father, but he would prove it to her. "But I will speak with her first."

"I wish you every success."

"Does this mean you now approve of me?"

Questions formed in Anthony's eyes. "I never

disapproved of you, Elliot, you are my best friend. I love you like a brother."

"Yet you did warn me away from her."

Anthony flushed. "Emma was an idealistic seventeen -year-old girl. You were different and had not been reared with the same gentility as us. Elliot, you would have terrified her. And then the accident happened…" his words trailed away, guilt and pain darkening his eyes. "It is my pain to bear for the rest of my life that my sister was horrifyingly hurt. I just wanted what was best for her."

"And I wasn't a duke then," he murmured, a peculiar weight in his heart.

"You cannot fault me, us, for wanting better for her. You had no wealth or status to keep her as she deserved."

"How unpleasant to know my worth as a husband for your sister was only measured by my purse and status and not my character, and not that I would have loved her beyond this life and the next," he said mildly.

Anthony frowned. "Emma never felt like that."

"I know."

"You do?"

"I asked her to marry me about six months after I became the duke of Hartford. She said a duke deserved better," he said gruffly. "But then she had been bound to a wheel chair."

"You never mentioned it," Anthony said. "Was it her rejections why you've hardly visited? You should have approached father. He would have formed a contract."

"Without her consent."

"Well yes, but—"

"I did not want her by force."

"I love you like a brother, and I do not give a damn about your past as you've insinuated before, but I care about Emma's future. I picture for her a doting husband, and children."

His mouth went dry at the very idea of her growing big with his child. "*If* that is what Emma wants, I can give it to her." The ache that filled him was crippling, it was a damn good thing his ass was already on the ground, or he would have fallen. "I've desired her for years," Elliot said without a hint of apology, "and I will crave her for a lifetime more."

Anthony nodded, looking sheepish, and then after a few moments held out his hand. Elliot took it, his heart somersaulting in his chest. This was the first time his friend had given any sign of approval that he would welcome a relationship between his best friend and sister.

"If Emma refuses, father will ensure she accepts. I must say you are the catch of the season."

Elliot went cold. "If Emma is even pricked, I will bury your father."

Anthony stiffened, ruthlessness shifting across his features. "Are you threatening my father?"

"Of course."

"Elliot—"

"No," he grounded. "Emma is his daughter. If he does anything to harm her, I will not show mercy. She is mine to protect, and that is what I will damn well do. I want to knock your teeth down your throat for even talking so casually about forcing her. Your job is also to protect her, at all costs. Even if it's from your father. He'll not do anything to force her. I'll ask, pray, cajole and hope she will say yes…but I'll never use force."

Anthony considered him coolly then nodded once, before mounting his horse and departing. Elliot remounted his horse and rode in the direction of his home. The vibrant green of the rolling countryside blurred by as he rode, feeling a sense of hope he hadn't felt in years. He envisioned Emma in his bed, by his side forever and his mouth went dry, and his heartbeat tripled.

He could not imagine a more perfect duchess, resilient in the face of such hardship, courageous enough to demand life had more to offer and seizing it with her sweet kindness.

Elliot smiled. He'd warned her, he'd told her to run, and she hadn't listened. He was going for her, and nothing would prevent him from claiming her as his duchess. How difficult that would be was another question he was willing to let simmer for another time.

CHAPTER 10

"His Grace, the duke of Hartford has called, Miss Emma."

"Yes…yes…I heard you the first time, Williams," she murmured to the hovering butler. "Have you informed the duke, Anthony has escorted Aunt Beatrice to Bath?"

"He has called for you, Miss Emma."

Emma took a deep breath. My goodness, she felt restless and out of sorts. The duke hadn't paid a personal call to her in years. Truly this could not be happenstance. Had Anthony betrayed her confidence?

"Have Mrs. Hodges send in tea and cakes. And please show in His Grace."

She felt very presentable in her high-waisted,

white-spangled gauze overdress with the palest green satin underskirt. Her hair had been coiffed in an elegant chignon with a few loose curls caressing her cheeks. Emma slowly stood as the duke strolled into the drawing room. Elliot had clearly ridden across to visit because he wore knee-high, dark brown, riding boots with gold tassels and breeches of tan moleskin that clung to his muscular thighs. He had discarded his riding crop, great coat, and his beaver but his jacket, waistcoat, and shirt were immaculate. Emma noticed that nestled in the folds of his cravat was a large gold set yellow diamond which reflected the glints in his golden eyes. No scenario she had imagined prepared her to see Elliot so soon after their night together. She hadn't thought she would have cause to see him before she sailed to see her sister Elizabeth. He was such a unique combination of casual power and refined elegance. She liked it, very much. Emma drank in all of him at once, and pleasure welled up from her stomach and burst upwards to her chest like sunshine. It was always so wonderful to see him but what was he doing there? *Please let it be a coincidence*, her heart could not bear anything else.

She directed an enquiring glance at him. "Elliot…I... I…Your Grace, I fear Anthony and

Maryann have left for Bath. They return in two days' time."

Sleek brows rose at her bumbling. Heat climbed her face, and she suddenly wished she had travelled down with them despite the ache in her leg and the pitying glances she had known she would receive. A bit flustered she dipped into a curtsy before lowering herself back on the sofa. His presence suddenly made the spacious and elegant drawing room seem compressed.

Mrs. Hodges bustled in with the tea trolley, and with quick bobs, she quietly departed.

"Forgive my abruptness, but what are you doing here, Elliot?"

His golden eyes ran over her like a physical caress. "Ah, I thought we were friends of sorts?"

Emma was instantly suspicious. More like petrified. She had written him every so often, and only received a few replies. She had sent him small tokens and gifts on his birthday and Christmas and received clipped thank yous. Friends did not ignore each other so.

His eyes lowered to the chess set on the small walnut table before her.

"You play yourself?"

"I…It is more enjoyable than it seems," Emma offered with a small wince. The fact she played herself was a testimony to how alone she was oftentimes.

"Are you well, Emma? You appear a bit flushed, and your eyes are very bright."

Silence met his polite inquiry.

A sensual smile curved his lips, knowledge gleamed in his eyes, and Emma wanted to die. *He knew.* Her heart which had already been warming up at seeing him decided to go for a trot and then a gallop. *Please let me be just overly anxious.*

"I have the most rotten headache this morning."

She gripped the teapot and tried to give him a small unconcerned smile. The dainty china trembled ever so slightly in her grasp. "Tea, Your Grace?"

His face became inscrutable at her formality. But she desperately needed the distance.

"No, thank you, Emma."

"Would you like a tart?"

"What I would like is for you to row on the lake with me, this afternoon perhaps?"

Elliot wanted to take her to rowing. A pastime they had enjoyed years past when life had been simple. So simple, but she saw the threat. "I always paint after luncheon," She said hoarsely.

"Would you make an exception?"

A lump grew in her stomach and spread to her throat. "I..."

His stare was unswerving but inscrutable. "I am sure you can make an exception. I was hoping we could talk. It has been a while."

She felt utterly wretched. This was not a coincidence. Anthony must have said something. She would kill her brother. She hated the slow fear and doubt that was snaking in her heart. "Elliot, your visit is so unexpected."

His smile was slow and somehow threatening. "I've missed you, our long walks across the countryside, swimming together, and our fencing."

Warmth spread throughout her body, but it wasn't enough to dispel the anxiety. "I think Anthony is still very displeased you taught me fencing."

The memory lingered between them, it had been a few days after her sixteenth birthday, and she had found him near the lake that separated her father's vast property from Elliot's humble cottage. His father had only recently died, and Elliot had looked so broken, sitting there with his knees to his chest and silent tears on his cheeks. That had been the first day she'd kissed him too, and tempted him from his melancholy by insisting she had always wanted to fence. He had happily or perhaps a bit desperately obliged, and many pleasant afternoons had passed by the lake with Elliot teaching her to fence.

How glorious those times had been. Suddenly the stately walls of her parents' country home felt as if they were beginning to close on her. Emma never did anything daring, not anymore. And she so wanted to, quite desperately. "I would like to go rowing," she said softly.

Surprise and pleasure flared in his eyes. He immediately stood and held out his hands.

Emma's eyes widened. Her teacup clattered loudly in the saucer, and it took her several seconds to recover. "Now?"

"Let's seize this rare and unmatched moment. I shan't give you the opportunity to change your mind."

Drat. He was right for her good sense was already reasserting itself. She stood, and collected her walking cane. "Shall we?"

She sucked in an audible breath at the brilliant heat that flared in his eyes. Several minutes later, they were walking along the path that would take them to the large lake that spanned for several miles. Her feet ached, and to her mortification, she stumbled a few times.

"Forgive me, Elliot, I—"

A surprised cry tore from her when he stepped behind her and swung her into his arms. "Your Grace, whatever are you doing?" she whispered furiously. He made no reply, and she gazed at him in uncertain silence. "What if we are seen?"

"By whom? The servants?" he said with such an unconcerned mien she wanted to slap him.

"Elliot put me down at once."

He stopped and peered down at her nestled in his arms. "Is your foot hurting?"

"Yes."

"Then it is my pleasure to carry you."

"We could go back for a curricle," she said with narrowed eyes. "Or my wheeled chair." The very idea burned along her nerve ending with discomfort.

His chin lifted toward the distance, and she turned her head.

"Can you see the lake, feel it beckoning to us?"

She swallowed, lifting her face to the gentle breeze that moved over the land. "Yes."

His expression became thoughtful. "Why waste time turning back when we're are almost there? My dear Emma, are you so alarmed to be in my arms?" His voice was very soft now.

At a loss for the proper response, she relaxed into his arms, and he continued walking ahead. Her arms gripped his shoulders, and she fought the need to get closer. He showed no sign of tiring, and she had to admire his endurance. A flush ran over her entire body as she recalled how tireless and insatiable he had been that night too. Dear God, she hoped he would not question the sudden brightness of her skin.

Finally, he set her down, and she shot him a disgruntled look.

"There are boats already on the lake. You seemed so sure, I would capitulate, weren't you?"

He looked back at her, his eyes alight with humor. "I was more hopeful."

They walked along the small boardwalk that stretched out into the waters. He went into the boat, and his hands grasped her waist to direct her as she began to move—clumsily, at first, then she was settled in quite comfortably. Elliot stripped off his coat and folded it neatly. Pleasure blasted through her that he had set oars for her as well.

That had always been one of the things she enjoyed so much about Elliot. He did not treat her as a delicate and helpless flower. She grabbed her oars, one in each arm and leaned back slightly a wide smile on her lips. He took up his, and they rowed.

It was peaceful, it was exhilarating, and a lump formed in her throat. "The last time I rowed was before the accident."

"I should have been back and—"

"No," she said with a smile, admiring the ripple of his muscles underneath his shirt with each push and pull of the oars. "I should have insisted Anthony take me, or ventured out myself."

He gave her a long, unreadable look. And how Emma wished she had the courage to ask why he had visited her now. Instead, she immersed herself in the tranquil beauty of the lake, exhilarating in the slight burn in the muscles of her arms as they rowed across the lake. It took several minutes to realize they were headed in the direction of the cottage he had lived in with his family.

"I haven't visited in a long time," he murmured at her searching glance.

"Is it occupied?"

"No…I bought it and have maintained it since."

Surprise shafted through her. "Why?"

His shoulder stiffened before his posture once more relaxed. "It is the only place where I see my parents. My father…my father was the second son, and he had fallen out of favor with his family for marrying my mother, and even for having the ambition of being a doctor. The first time I saw Glenhaven Manor, my country seat in Kent, it seized my breath. There are over two hundred rooms, and it sits among thousands of acres. There is a gallery of family paintings, and only one shows my father when he was a lad of about twelve. It was as if he was eradicated."

"How awful," she breathed, suddenly wishing she had been there for him while he navigated a world that must have been so new and unsettling.

He gently steered the boat toward the next gangplank, and they lowered their oars. Elliot efficiently tied up the boat and assisted her out. The humble but well-tended house loomed over a small hill.

"In those early days, I would come back here often and just sit in the dark in the parlor. Sometimes I would stay for a few days and then return to London or wherever my grandmother thought I needed to be to learn how to be a duke."

A gust of wind swept over the land, and she pressed her hand atop her head to keep her bonnet in place, while the other gripped her walking cane.

"I've heard of the dowager duchess. She is said to be fearsome and terribly influential. It is said even Beau Brummel feared her, before his exile of course," Emma said with a light laugh.

"A veritable dragon," Elliot said with an undertone of admiration.

Emma gasped as he swung her into his arms and started along the path which inclined over the small hill. The pleasure of him holding her was too great, and the awareness she would like to be in his arms forever surged through her heart.

The surrounding gardens which his mother had been proud of, burst with wild beauty. He lowered Emma to her feet at the top of the hill, his hands ran lightly over her sides, lingering just beneath her arms. They glanced down at the cottage.

She glanced up at him. "Would you like to go inside?"

He touched her face fleetingly, his finger leaving a trail of warmth across her cheek. "Will you come with me?"

That brief intimate touched left her flustered and too aware of the man standing before her, looking at her with such tenderness. She caught her lower lip between her teeth, and his gaze sharpened on that telling action.

"I…"

"I won't bite," he said with some amusement, his golden eyes so watchful.

Huffing, she grabbed her cane and walked carefully down the incline, ignoring his soft laughter. At times she bent and inhaled the fragrance of several flowers—jasmine, hyacinth, lilies, and daffodils. The countryside during springtime was her favorite time of the year.

They made their way toward the cottage door, and he inserted an iron key into the lock. The door was pushed open, and he stepped back so she could precede him inside. Emma stepped across the threshold and faltered. Nothing had changed. The striped wallpaper which decorated the walls of the hallway and the patterning of trellised roses in the parlor was the same as she remembered. Everything was as it had been when Elliot's father had been alive although perhaps a little better cleaned and maintained. She ambled toward the ajar door of the small but tastefully furnished parlor and smiled. Even here had been preserved, and a fire was already lit. It was a cozy room, functional and without pretension to grandeur. The mantel held a few cheerful pottery ornaments, such as could be picked up for sixpence at a country fair.

"There is someone here?"

"I sent word I was coming down, but we are alone."

She faced him. "I cannot help but feel you wanted me to come here with you today."

"I did."

"I wonder what you would have done had I refused to row with you," she said teasingly, not liking the shaken feeling low in her stomach.

"I confess I wanted privacy, but if you had refused, we would have had this conversation back at Bellview manor."

"You have me at a disadvantage, for what do you require privacy?"

Piercing eyes regarded her thoughtfully. He dipped his hands into his inner breast pocket of his jacket and withdrew the delicate eye mask she had worn to Lady Waverly's masquerade ball. "You left this."

How effortlessly he destroyed her. Her defenses had been laid bare and the considerable ease at which he had done it made her itch to slap his face. Emma had not even realized sometime throughout their long night she had lost it. She allowed a small unaffected smile to curve her lips. It felt like the hardest thing she had ever done in her life. "And you ventured all this way to deliver this to me? Unnecessary but curious."

Appreciation and challenge lit his eyes. "Curious indeed. On my ride over, I devised numerous ways in how to get you to admit the truth. I am a bit disappointed I won't get to torture you after all," he drawled, eyes dipping to the pulse fluttering frantically at her throat.

She put her cane on the sofa, and folded her arms across her stomach, hoping he did not see it for the defensive move it was. "I cannot imagine what you are thinking now. I do not know why Anthony thought he had to betray my confidence. I never intended to put you in such a position, Elliot I want you to forget last night ever happened."

"I wonder, why did your heart tremble the instance I entered the drawing room?"

She gaped at him, blushing furiously. "It did not."

He remained silent, but his eyes glittered with cool knowledge, mocking her. Mortifyingly her nipples beaded under his gaze, and the flesh beneath her legs heated. *Dear God.* "It was only one night, and I had…have no intention of repeating the encounter."

"I can take you now, without preliminaries, and you would scream for me, loving every pounding thrust or gentle glide, Emma."

Fear snaked through her, and arousal stabbed into the heart of her at his words. He was the most sinfully alluring man she'd ever met, and somehow, he knew how she reacted to him. After their night together, he would not be in doubt. Her arousal dampened between her thighs with shocking speed, and she fought to keep her face blank. "You could try, but I would not allow it. I do not want more than the one night we had, Elliot."

He stiffened. "Why?"

"Why what?"

"Why do you only wish for one night with me?"

The question made her chest ache.

He leaned his hips against the mantle by the fireplace, his stare unswerving. Was it that he wanted more than one night? Her mind dismissed the possibility. Yet after a few seconds, she arrived at the same conclusion. The idea was so preposterous, so frightfully appealing she glared at him for eliciting the powerful need, excitement, and doubt mashing painfully together inside.

"What do you want from me?" she whispered instead of answering his question. *I know your intent to marry…*

"Did you not declare to Anthony your plans to court Lady Andrea. The *perfect* debutante of this season?"

A frown chased his features. "I have no intention to court her or anyone else. I know the woman I want to spend the rest of my life with if she will grant me the honor."

Emma stared at him with a mixture of dread and fascination, and a peculiar weight filled her heart, and a lump grew in her throat. "I ask again, Your Grace, what do you want from me?"

Somehow, she got the impression he was nervous, and that was an even more preposterous idea. Elliot Winthrop was never nervous. He had grown into the poise and confidence of a nobleman who was well aware of his worth in society.

"More," he said softly.

Emma swallowed. "More of what?"

He stepped closer, and she moved back. He faltered, but his eyes never left hers. "More of you, more than one night, forever."

She put some safe distance between them, anger whipping through her blood. "Why are you saying this? You haven't paid any addresses to me in eight years."

He glared at her, seemingly waging an internal war. "Did you want me to?"

Yes…no. "If you had wanted me, why did you stay away for so long?"

"Staying away from you has been the hardest thing I've ever done. You rejected my offer of marriage *three* times…and my heart and pride were wounded. Each letter you sent to me was a twisting knife in an open wound that had no chance of healing. I had to distance myself from you to preserve my sanity. I never thought I had another chance with you until you came to the masquerade ball."

The air heated and tension arched from him to her.

"I've stayed away over the years…but I will not continue to do so. Please give me a chance."

After years of hopeless longing to hear such renewed sentiments, how strange his expressions did not fill her with relief, more like despair. "No." Her refusal sounded so weak. Wanting to be firm she squared her shoulders and lifted her chin.

"Why not?"

"If I had not come to you last night, would you have ever approached me?" she asked softly.

He shielded his eyes, but not before she saw the flash of guilt and torment.

"Eventually I would have come for you."

She stared at him in ill-concealed disbelief. "You expect me to believe this? You have only been a shadow in my life since the last time you made an offer, that was eight years ago Elliot, only a few months after you became a duke. And I know why you stayed away, it was because your offer for marriage had been out of pity for my circumstances."

The soft rhythm of his breathing fractured. "Emma, each time I visited, no matter how briefly was about seeing *you*, always you. Every single visit was about being near to you, seeing your smile and laughter, being a part of your happiness, sharing your doubts and fears. Last night…last night you destroyed my world and restraints from simply pressing your lips to mine. Last night inspired me to hope for a forever with you, because you turned to me, Emma."

She held up ineffectual hands, hoping to stem the tide of words that she knew had the power to break her, but he continued, "I stayed away because you were convinced you were broken, that I could not manage your pain and hopes, that I did not love you enough to see *you*. You've shown me you crave me as much as I yearn for you."

Her breath hitched. *Please stop talking*, her heart screamed. His words were a massive hammer to her resistance. "I have always wanted you, Elliot, you know that. Last night was wonderful for me, and I will cherish the memory forever. But I only did it because I thought it would remain my secret. I simply wanted a night for me, to indulge in desires I have long held, and I chose to have that experience with someone I knew and trusted. I never realized you *knew*."

"So, you only wanted to use me?"

"Use you?" She searched his face wildly. Emma hoped he did not believe her capable of treating him so callously. Anger burned through her. He had easily succumbed to her charms and had taken her more thoroughly than she had used him. "Who was taking advantage of whom, Elliot? Within less than half an hour I was in your bed. If Anthony had not gabbed to you…you would not even know that it was me."

"Is that what you believe of me? That I easily take women I do not know to my bed? I recognized you the moment you stepped into the ballroom, Princess."

The breath rushed from her lungs, and with sickening clarity, Emma knew he had known. He had referred to her more than once as princess…in that same mocking tone he had always used. She had not been overly paranoid this morning when the awareness had settled in her heart.

"*You knew?*" She could not wrap her thoughts around his revelation. My goodness, but it made sense. Her conquest had been easy. The tenderness she felt from him at times, the gentle way he had cleaned her after. Even when he had ridden her hard, testing her limits, he had seemed so wonderfully sweet. He had been gentle, caring, soothing, and her heart had tripped in her chest in wonder, pain, and jealousy. Thinking he was this way with all his lovers. "Oh God." She suppressed the joy that tried to swarm her.

His expression became guarded. "Why are you so afraid?"

He made no move toward her as if he knew she was on the verge of panicking and running. But she could see the control in which he encased himself. Her heart thumped a frantic tattoo against her breastbone. She lowered herself into the sofa, refusing to meet his gaze. "I am not afraid."

"You are. The woman behind the mask was not a façade. She was not timid or repressed. She was bold and delightfully wicked. She took what she wanted. That woman was *you*, Emma. You took me. And you are not allowed to hide and retreat to the tidy and risk-free life your parents have placed you in."

Shock roared through her, making her light-headed. Her lashes dipped. She wanted him to see her, but not too deep. "What do you want from me, Elliot?" She splayed her hands wide. "We both have wanted each other for years…and now that we have tasted of each other, we can move on with our lives."

"Wrong," he grounded out with enough force to have her surging to her feet once more. "You think after you have come to me…after you have shown me that you want me as much as I need you, I would ever allow you to leave the possibility of us?"

Her eyes widened. Allow? Fire sparking in her veins, she stalked toward him and jabbed him in the chest. The soft smile on his lips only infuriated her further. "Allow? I am tired of people telling me what I can and cannot do. I have the power to make *my* choice. No one will allow me anything!"

He advanced, backing her up until she was flush against the arm of the sofa. "Then why do you *allow* your parents to cage you from living, why are you running away from England?" he asked with a quiet intensity. "Why do you allow your fears to control your future?"

Her heart executed a sick flip of alarm. He saw too deep inside of her. She craned her neck to look at him. How could she make him understand? He was her one night of passion. Her stolen moment. He was this beautiful fire she'd stepped too close to, and she was miraculously alive, and not singed to death. He was too overwhelming for her to be with for any period of time. He was a duke, and he would be expected to provide an heir, he would require a wife who was perfect and flawless to host his political parties, balls, and dinners. Elliot had always been so adventurous. Once they had ridden across the lanes, fenced, swam together. Everything had changed, and she was so limited now. Her life was now safe and predictable, and she liked it being that way. Elliot was dangerous and uncertain…now an exotic creature she could never hope to hold onto for any length of time. "I am not running."

His narrowed gaze skimmed over her with renewed intensity. "Is that so?"

Her heart thudded, but she pressed on. "Yes. I am different now. A great night for me is curling by the fire and reading a book. I find joy in walking through the park with my sketchpad and capturing the beauty of life. I love riding gently in the country. I do not love the parties, and the glamorous life of the *ton*."

He frowned, eyes searching her face. He cupped her face. His shoulder relaxed, and he closed his eyes with a sigh. "Emma?"

"Yes?"

"Marry me."

Her entire body trembled.

He dipped his head and leaned in close, so their lips almost touched, their nose brushing. "Let me prove you are the only woman I want. Have ever needed. Marry me, my darling."

The need to scream 'yes' welled inside her. "I… I may never be able to have a child. The doctors said—"

"I do not mean to dismiss your fears or pain, but the doctors also said you would never walk again. If we are not so blessed, we will comfort each other, but it is you I want, Emma, *you*."

"But your dukedom—"

His thumb dragged roughly over her bottom lip. She caught it between her teeth and bit lightly. Not quite believing her own shameless intentions, she tried to step back. He did not allow her. He tugged her to him, and she willingly went.

"I did not expect this, Elliot. I never imagined—"

He pressed a kiss to her forehead, and her heart clenched, then melted. She fought to shore up her resolve. Though she badly wanted to say yes, it would be a grave mistake. One she would probably never be able to recover from.

"Say yes, Emma."

She gently disengaged from him and tilted her head to meet his eyes. The need that glittered there tempted her to step off the cliff of insanity. "I can't," she breathed roughly. The doubts and fears had held her too long, for them to be so easily dismissed. She did not want to accept his proposal without careful consideration. How could he blithely dismiss his duty to the title? He would need an heir and a capable duchess by his side. A smile slanted his wide sensual mouth, turning his hard-edged masculinity to a charming male. "Do you have any idea how much I've wanted you?"

She shook her head, unable to speak lest she betrayed the need pumping in her blood, and beating between her legs for him.

"I've craved you, Emma. For years. Be honest with me, how much do you want me?"

The words slipped unbidden from her lips. "You threaten all the beliefs I hold about my expectations for my life. You make me burn to live."

Approval flared in his gaze, then his lips took hers, and Emma stopped breathing. His dark head lowered over hers, he kissed her. His tongue slipped past her lips, swept over hers, and arousal burned through her. He got her wet so fast, Emma was almost embarrassed.

He pulled her against him, seducing her mouth with scorching expertise. She was painfully aware of the hard bulge against her stomach, and how secluded they were. He broke away from her mouth to bite the side of her neck. She whimpered, overwhelmed by the pleasure darting through her.

He stumbled onto the sofa, and she went with him, climbing onto his lap, arousal, need, and his hands directing her. *No.* She screamed inside, knowing her kissing him did not mean she was caving, but she was unable to stop licking his lips, to stop thrusting her hands through his thick hair.

His fingers encircled her ankles, and pushed up, sliding against her stockings and taking her dress with it. Sensual weakness assailed her. He wrapped an arm beneath her hips, lifted her, and positioned her over his thick length. *When had he opened his flap?* His fingers traced the swollen folds of her cleft, and Emma gasped against his mouth as he parted her swollen flesh. He drew her down to meet the surge of his hip. She bit down on his bottom lip as he pulled her down. Though she was wet and welcoming the tight stretch was almost painful. A garbled whimper tore from her throat as his thrust impaled her deep and hard. She couldn't speak, couldn't breathe, and couldn't think, only feel. "*Elliot.*"

He began a slow, rocking motion. "Emma, my darling, ride me," he ordered roughly.

Lust poured through her bloodstream, heating her from the inside out as she obeyed his command and rode him. Her knees bracketed his hips as she, at first, very clumsily, and then with more grace moved up and down his length, controlling the pace, the burn, wanting them to conflagrate slowly. He gripped her hips and buried his mouth in her throat with a deep groan as she clenched on him.

"Ride harder." His words were a guttural snarl, his eyes narrowed with need.

His dark golden eyes burned with passion, searing away the slow control she wanted to take him with.

"No," she said, and took his bottom lip between her teeth again and nipped. *Hard.*

The moan that slipped from him inflamed her. Sensual power tunneled through Emma, and she slid down with excruciating slowness over his thick length. His hands tightened on her hips as his eyes narrowed even further. She almost smiled at the carnal grimace that twisted his lips as she rolled her hips, clenching her walls and bearing down on his cock, even slower than before.

"You are fucking with fire," he muttered, his voice filled with need.

The crude word sent a flush though her entire body. She gripped his hair, tunneling her finger through his strands, feeling his scalp under her fingertips. "Strange, my duke, I thought I was taking *you*," she whispered, her lips touching the underside of his jaw.

His gaze burned into hers, and as she watched the fight for control, sweet power shifted inside of her along with need. She had thought she would never have felt his wildness again, this daring to be free. But something about now was even *more* than the night before. *He knows it's me.* Her throat burned, and tears pricked behind her lids.

"Sweet mercy," he said, kissing her like a starving man.

Emma gasped and clutched his shoulders tightly. He made love to her mouth, and she rocked on him with exquisite slowness, but with depth. With such depth, her core ached, and her nub burned for release. He stood with her and spun, gently lowering her onto the sofa, but never releasing her. They remained like that, only kissing, but she could feel him getting harder inside of her though he was not thrusting. She squirmed, wanting him to move, but he only ravished her mouth. She had no other way to describe the deep thrust and curl of his tongue against hers. He was making love to her mouth, mating their tongues together, burning them alive with desire. Emma whimpered at the sharpness of the pleasure rising in her.

They pulled apart, breathing raggedly. His face suddenly took on a look of cruel sensuality as he looked at her. Their night of passion at the masquerade ball swirled in his gaze, and the memory of the ways he had taken her crawled through her.

"Elliot," she whimpered, nervous despite the delirious pleasure filling her. He was so wonderfully intense.

Her eyes widened as he dragged her to the edge of the sofa. He lifted one of her feet and placed it on the edge of the sofa, while her other foot hitched at his hips. There was only the slightest pinch along her muscles of her leg. The position splayed her wide, and as she looked down, she could see where they were joined. Heat suffused her face, and her heart raced. He pulled from her until he was poised at her entrance. She clenched, feeling empty, wanting to be filled with him.

"Look at me."

She met his intense gaze as he thrust into her in one smooth lunge. The hard, abrupt impalement had her crying out at the sensuous burn.

"Hold me, Emma."

She slipped her hands around his neck. Before she could draw another breath, his hips recoiled, and he slammed into her hard and deep. She wailed against his kisses. A sound that shocked her. Not even last night she had sounded so broken with lust. Within seconds, he commanded a deep, powerful rhythm that had her gripping him and panting for breath. Emma lost herself, to pleasure, to need, to lust. "Don't stop," she moaned. "Please don't stop."

"Never," he promised.

The perfect blend of bliss and pain as he took her had Emma shuddering and shaking as coils of need raked at her, shattering all control she had long abandoned.

"I love you, Emma," he whispered against her lips.

Joy soared through her along with blinding doubt. Delirious pleasure swept through Emma as she shattered, and she rode the sweet wave of ecstasy trembling and moaning. With a deep groan, he thrust one more time and then tumbled with her.

"I cannot marry you, Elliot."

It was probably not the most romantic thing to say after what they just shared, but it was blaring from her mind.

He stiffened, then cursed. He pulled from her, withdrew his handkerchief from his top pocket and cleaned her. Heat crawled up her neck. How difficult it was to meet his eyes.

"You could be with my child now," he said softly.

Their gazes collided.

Tears filled her eyes as she stared up at him, trembling, terrified and hopeful in equal measure that he could be right. "Th…the doctors," she stammered. "We—"

He reached for her hand and squeezed it. "Hang the doctors. Anything is possible."

God, what have I done? Why was it so easy to be free with him?

She pulled out of his grip, refusing to meet his gaze as she swiped at the tears that escaped her control and fell from her eyes.

"What must I do to convince you?" he said finally, quietly.

She bit her lip, trying to stem the shaking of her heart. He was so tall and broad, his body leanly muscled and graceful. And she very much wanted to just lean on him after their earlier passion. "Please take me home," she said thickly, her heart thundering in her chest. The familiar comfort of her room was where she needed to be, to simply think.

His eyes flared before they went distant. "I see. I never realized you were such a coward, Emma."

She felt ridiculously vulnerable and afraid. She was standing rather stiffly, her hands clasped tightly in front of her, struggling against the doubts inside and the fear. "I would shame you," she whispered. "Most days I still use a wheel chair, and I fear I will forever need one. There are good days, but those are less than the bad ones. Sometimes the pain in my leg is so bad, I will be abed for hours. I am still broken, and I fear I will never be whole."

"Why do you allow your circumstances to define you and the possibility of us?"

"I only protect my heart from the pain of your eventual pity and derision. Of your eventual resentment if I am unable to provide you with an heir. The doctors said with the back pain I've suffered from the accident and still suffer, even if I were to fall with child, I might never carry that child to full term."

His face went blank, but not before she saw the flash of raw emotions in the depth of his eyes. Emma's breath hitched, and her heart slammed into her throat.

"Do you truly think my love, admiration, and respect would be so inconstant? Do you think I am so puffed with vanity of myself and my position in society that I cannot adore and admire the woman you are, as you are? Do you think me so without substance and heart?"

The sudden emotional distance shook her. "I did not mean it like that, Elliot."

"Then how did you mean it?"

Perceiving that she had offended his pride and possibly wounded his heart, she made no reply, for her throat was too tight. A muscle jumped in his jaw at her silence, then a smile of icy disdain curled his lips.

"I understand now, Emma. I'll not bother you by renewing obviously unwanted and distressing sentiments."

His words shattered something deep inside of her, and the indifference in his voice flayed her.

"I will see you home."

They left, and she walked ahead at a jerky pace. Her legs knotted, and she stumbled, and then strong arms were about her as he lifted and walked with her toward the boat bobbing atop the placid water. Emma cried unashamedly. His eyes held a piercing sadness as he stared at her, and she was vaguely conscious that her throat was slightly raw. They made it to the boat and settled in. She could not row, only sobbed.

"Elliot…" She stuffed a fist in her mouth, not understanding the tearing pain ripping through her heart. His eyes were so indifferent. As he rowed, he watched her as though he waited for something. And she had no notion what.

Today had shown her so much what their life could be like, what she had always dreamed it could be, fun, sensual, an entwining of souls. She wanted to see his face each night before she fell asleep, and she wanted to wake nestled in his arms. If only that were possible.

"You will let me know if you find yourself with child."

Fear and hope darted through her in equal measure.

"If you are we *will* marry…for the sake of our child."

She nodded mutely. Her despair deepened, and she rested her forehead on her knees and wept for losing what she had so badly desired for so many years, but had been too terrified to reach for.

CHAPTER 11

Elliot stood in the forecourt of Bellview Manor and watched as the door gently closed on Emma's retreating back, his chest tight, his heart racing. She'd said no...*again*. He'd been prepared for her rejection, but it still hurt like a brutal punch to his gut. It had been a mistake to touch her, to smell her, to taste her skin, and slide into her, to take pleasure from her. How she had taken him just now had been the most satisfying experience of Elliot's life, yet the most hollow and heartrending. Emma's eyes offered everything to him and promised nothing. He never thought it possible to feel the emotional pain that had cut into him like a knife just now. He tried to reason around the awful feelings seething in his gut and could find no relief. What a fool he had been to think her coming to him at the masquerade meant more. What a fool he had been to allow her back into his heart after all the years of rejection. Elliot sheathed his emotions in ice, burying the disappointment burning in his gut.

Every instinct clamored for him to barge into the manor, snatch her into his arms and never let her go. Instead, he turned and moved toward the stables, calling for his horse. He would have to let her go. It was impossible to fight for someone who would forever push him away. Enough was enough. Yet the very notion of truly losing her settled against his heart like a boulder. He faltered, slapping his hand against his forehead, lifting his face to the sky, desperately seeking the warmth of the sun to melt the cold, hollow knot of loss wrapping around his heart.

It was difficult to move, to breathe, to imagine a future without her, to think clearly. Cursing his weakness, he mounted his horse and rode home, blanking everything from his thoughts, only feeling the wind on his face as he rode. Several hours later he rested at an inn, where his assurance it was not necessary prevented the proprietor from trying to remove a couple with their children from the establishment's best room. Elliot took a much simpler room with a narrow cot and tried to sleep. He failed abysmally. He could find no peace.

After another few hours of restlessness, he departed the inn and continued towards his estates. He rode through the night, the cold nipping at his bones, his superfine jacket inadequate protection against the chill of the night. But he was undaunted and continued traveling, thankful for once since he'd left Emma, visions of her did not haunt him.

The sun had risen, and lit the land in rays of sunshine when Elliot arrived at Glenhaven Manor quite surprised to see at least six ladies strolling across the lawns, their parasols open to protect their delicate skin from the sun. He handed his horse over to the stables and made his way to the main house. The butler, Andrews, opened the door before Elliot knocked. He faltered as the gentle playing of a pianoforte echoed through the long hallway of the manor.

"Andrews, what is going on?"

The butler cleared his throat. "The duchess is in residence, along with a few young ladies, Your Grace."

He handed over his top hat, and then made his way to the parlor. His grandmother did not reside with him at Glenhaven, at least not since she'd opened the dower house over two years past. Nor did she arrive without informing him, nor did she extend invitations to ladies to visit his home.

Reaching the drawing room, he pushed wider the ajar door and stepped inside.

"Grandmother."

The chattering ceased, and four pairs of hopeful eyes turned in his direction. He was familiar with Lady Felicity, and Lady Olivia, both ladies from estimable families. The other two ladies seemed familiar, but their name escaped him at the moment. His grandmother stood, her lips firmly pinched, but there was some measure of a smile in her eyes.

Was she pleased to see him? Strange that, for she was an utterly humorless lady.

Swift introductions were made, and the ladies dipped into elegant curtseys. Their eyes held hope and expectations he did not understand, and a sliver of alarm went through him. His grandmother deftly and delicately dismissed the lot, and Elliot closed the door as the last lady exited.

"What is going on?" he asked without preamble.

She sat in the chair closest to the windows, her

cane clasped in her hand, appearing like a queen on her throne. Her chin lifted. "These are the leading young ladies from the ten finest families in London. I've signaled your intention to select a wife by inviting them to Glenhaven Manor, you will select a wife from one of these ladies," she said imperiously.

"I beg your pardon?"

"I am partial to Lady Lavinia, she is very accomplished and poised, well-mannered and genteel. Plays the pianoforte with admirable skills, and her needle point is excellent."

"I see."

"You will sit beside her at tonight's dinner, and you will signal your interest which she will be very grateful and—"

Elliot laughed. His grandmother scowled, and never had he seen a more ferocious image. "Forgive my unexpected humor, I meant no insult. I simply had an unexpected realization."

"One you will no doubt share," she said frostily.

"It is always honorable and worthwhile to fight for that which is worthy," Elliot murmured. "A notion my father taught me from as early as I can recall, and I seemed to have forgotten it over the years. I do hope they will not suffer any embarrassment when I send the ladies home. I am not interested in marrying any of them."

She surged to her feet. "What nonsense. You must marry and produce an heir."

"I hope with my heart I will have that happiness."

A frown chased her brows, and golden eyes narrowed. "You are the duke of—"

"Of Hartford, I know," he murmured. "I will marry no other woman while I love another."

His words settled into the fraught silence. Elliot placed a hand on his chest. He'd not know he would have made that admission, and inexplicably it felt gloriously right. "I love Miss Emma Fitzgerald, with all parts of me. I've loved her for ten years, and I have foolishly let my pride stand in the way of chasing her."

His grandmother's eyes widened in evident shock. "Chase her?" she whispered furiously. "You are the duke of—"

"Of Hartford, I know, I suppose all the ladies of society are supposed to fall at dukes' feet, and we do not pursue them?"

Her outrage was apparently too great for a rebuttal.

"I love Emma Fitzgerald," he said again. "I've

finally allowed myself to imagine a life with her, and I cannot let her go. She does not want me, in fact, I offered for her yesterday, and she rejected me, for the fourth time."

Profound relief glared from the duchess's eyes. "Sensible girl, she is unsuitable."

"I should never have left," he said, walking toward his grandmother to stand in front of her. "I foolishly left her when she needed me the most. A wounded animal fights those who try to help them, and I never realized that's what Emma did. She was hurt, profoundly, and the more I pushed to be there for her, to make her my wife so I would always be there for her, the more she pushed me away. I gave up on her," he said hoarsely, unashamed of the burning in his eyes. "I gave up on her, and I never saw it, I gave up on *us*."

His grandmother remained stiff and disapproving, but he did not care.

"I will never give up on her again or on our love. If she travels to America, I will take a ship and follow her. I am but a shadow of the man I want to be without her, and I suspect, she is just as wounded without me."

He bent and pressed a kiss to his grandmother's papery cheek. Elliot smiled wryly at her shock.

"Thank you, Grandmother, for thinking of my future. But I'll marry no woman unless it is Emma Fitzgerald."

Then he turned and exited the drawing room, planning his campaign to win his love.

Emma reposed on the chaise in her room, gazing through the window, not seeing the wild beauty of the land in springtime. At first, she'd cried, then did some gentle stretches on her leg, then read, anything to wrest her mind from the tormenting memories of the last few days, but the pain and tension had not dissipated.

Three days had passed since she saw him last, and it felt like a lifetime.

She had refused him out of sheer fear he would find her lacking. That when he saw the mess of scars on her legs, she would see pity in his eyes. She was a damn coward. Saying it in the most disparaging way she could think of did not make her feel better. She was truly aching down to her bones. All she could see was the raw flash of pain in Elliot's eyes. It haunted her. She'd hurt him when he deserved nothing of the kind. Earlier he'd looked at her as if he loved her with every part of his soul.

Oh, Elliot.

She'd only spent a few hours with him and had been branded, and she wanted a lifetime more. A knock sounded on her door, and she jerked.

"Yes?" It was impossible to soften the abrupt nature of her demand. Partly because of her turmoil over Elliot, and partly because she had insisted her parents not invade her space after having to assert her right to privacy when they had bombarded her earlier. Mamma and papa had been fueled by Aunt Beatrice's fanciful account of Emma's attendance to Lady Waverly's ball.

"It's Maryann," her sister said before opening the door and entering.

She waddled over, her stomach seeming impossibly larger in the couple days she had been gone. "When you did not come down for luncheon I felt concerned. Is all well?"

"I…yes."

"Your eyes are suspiciously puffy and red," Maryann said climbing atop the bed and reclining against a few pillows.

"The duke visited while you were in Bath."

"Oh dear."

"He knew it was me…at the masquerade ball."

Maryann's eyes widened, quite dramatically. "Upon my word, however did he discover?"

"He said," Emma cleared her throat, and shifted from the windows to face her sister. "He said he knew it was me, the moment he saw me." She closed her eyes, tilting her head onto the cushion. "I've missed him so, Maryann. He is different. Harder, more elegant, he wears authority like a second skin."

"Well he is a duke now," her sister said archly. "The dowager duchess's tutelage would have been thorough."

"I want to know the man he is today." Emma hungered for the long walks, the reading by the fire, playing chess, and then the wicked kisses. "When he told Anthony of his intention to marry, I do not believe the duke thought I was a candidate. My heart is so afraid it is because of my wounds he didn't seem to reconsider me, but I must logically think it was because I rejected his offer of marriage three times."

Maryann gasped. "I thought he only approached papa once."

"The other two were private meetings between

the duke and I." It was impossible she could fall more in love with him.

"Emma, you are crying." She gasped, raising her hands to her cheeks.

"What is it?" Maryann's voice was low and undemanding.

"He has renewed his sentiments, and I said no once more…but I wanted to say *yes*."

"You are afraid."

"Yes."

"I must say I've never thought you would be afraid of anything," Maryann said softly. "You were so brave after the accident. How you fought to walk, to live, how you never gave up hope. I never realized you were frightened to love."

Emma swallowed past the tight knot in her throat. "Yes." She laughed shakily. "And how very silly it is of me, for I have lost him. I never had him, for I never gave him a chance."

"Do you love him?" Maryann asked, sympathy glowing from her eyes.

"More than anything else. And I have done so for years. I want him with everything in me. He rouses my passion, my joy for life," she said, a flush rising in her face. The weight that lifted from her shoulders on her declaration was glorious.

"It sounds like you already know the answer to your fears, Emma."

Maryann pushed from the bed, ambled over and pressed a kiss to her cheek. "Do not dawdle too long."

"I will never be right for him regardless of how I feel."

Maryann stared at her with a mess of emotions on her face, but she remained silent.

Elliot, I miss you. Oh, to be in his arms again. Emma ached with exquisite longing. A state she would forever exist in once Elliot was not by her side. She closed her eyes allowing the memories of the years gone by to wash over her senses. She had always shied away from them, hating how they reminded her of the broken, hollow creature she had been. She had been bedridden for months, and the doctors had held no hope she would ever walk again. But why hadn't she made an effort to see him once she had healed? Why hadn't she trusted in the love that shone from his eyes?

She allowed all the memories to wash over her, the pity from her family, the sobs of her mother, how invalided she had felt, their refusal to assist her to relearn to walk, insisting she should listen to the doctors and not her own stubborn heart. Only her sisters had aided her in the secret of their rooms. If her family had loved her and had been so ashamed of her, how could Elliot have borne it?

She covered her mouth, her eyes staring sightlessly out the windows. How could she have judged him by their standards, how she had had been convinced all her doubts had been justified when he hadn't returned to court her again? Emma had never been a coward, and it hurt, soul deep, that she had been afraid to love for so long.

THE VERY NEXT day a single white rose was delivered to her. Emma knew it was from the duke, and the relief that had surged through her heart had been telling. There had been so many questions in her heart, so many doubts as to her suitability when he had not renewed his sentiments. And those doubts had only cemented over the years to a sort of acceptance that he too must have realized she would not be worthy of being his duchess.

The second day a book of poetry by John Keats arrived.

The third day a pair of silken stockings arrived, a shocking present for a man to send to an unmarried woman and they were not even formally engaged. If her parents discovered the gift, they would demand that she return them. A dangerous thrill had burst in her heart at his scandalous gift. And on the fourth day, he sent a song of some sort, a terrible rude one, but it made a laugh hiccup from her. With trembling fingers, she had folded the paper as if it were precious and stored it in the top drawer of her writing desk. The fifth day she got a pearl seeded comb for her hair with the most elegant design.

The sixth day a personal invitation to a ball arrived from Lady Sterling, and Emma knew it was the duke's influence which had allowed it to happen. Her family had not been invited to that auspicious event in years. In fact, Emma couldn't recall if they had ever been to Lady Sterling's annual spring ball. Her mother would be overjoyed.

And then she would adamantly insist Emma was not to attend.

She must comport herself accordingly and never shame the family. Those had been the stringent repeated words of her mamma and papa since her carriage accident. She hadn't attended the theater, never visited Covent Garden, or attended any rout parties. Comporting herself correctly according to her mother had been to hide from society, not bringing the polite world's attention to the fact the viscount and viscountess Sherwood had a crippled daughter.

It was not any concerns for her wellbeing that had urged her family to retire in Cheswick Manor. It had been their mortification. Emma closed her eyes, for she too had been responsible for the prison in which she had dwelt. For so many years she had been content with hiding in the country, forsaking all the elegance, companionship, entertainment and extravagance of the *ton*.

Squaring her shoulders, she knocked once on the drawing room door, then opened it and stepped in. Her family had been gathered at her request. Her papa sat in a high wing backed chair by the fireplace, and her mother and Aunt Beatrice sat on the chaise, Maryann was curled in a single sofa, her feet lifted onto an ottoman, and Anthony lingered by the windows overlooking the lake.

"Emma, dearest, dinner will be served by seven and—" her mother's words broke off, and she gaped.

Her father stood frowning, no doubt trying to distinguish what about her was different.

"Where is your cane?" he boomed, making his

way over, to only falter as Anthony exclaimed, "What happened to your hair?"

Emma smiled. With the aid of Maryann and her maid, Emma had cut her hair in the first style of fashion. Her mamma's eyes widened with incredulity, and her papa seemed terribly flustered. Even Anthony seemed nonplussed by her transformation. Aunt Beatrice for once seemed at a loss for words, and only Maryann smiled with pleasure.

"Dear brother, please close your mouth," Emma said with a gentle smile.

"Upon my word, what have you truly done to your hair," Aunt Beatrice gasped in her dramatic fashion. "All your glorious locks, all gone."

Emma's head felt lighter and freer, the angles of her cheeks seemed more angular and sensual, now that her hair went no longer than the curve of her cheeks. "I've also ordered a new wardrobe for the upcoming season."

Mamma looked ready to faint.

"I intend to book passage next week to America, and I'll sail at the end of the season. I will visit with Elizabeth for several months. I will write often, I promise," she said softly."

A frown snapped between her father's brows. "I

believe Anthony has mentioned I've given Lord Coventry's permission—"

"Forgive the interruption, papa," she said firmly. "I will not be marrying the earl. I am five and twenty, and I flatter myself that I can direct my life, with your guidance when I find I need. I have never been to a ball," she whispered, her throat suddenly tight with the ache of all she had missed. "I never attended the races, even Maryann has visited the opera. I've been told for years, by *all* of you, in varied forms, I am not ready to face society. I allowed myself to believe it, to accept your guidance because I was so very afraid of pity and condescending attitudes, and spiteful remarks. I was so busy being afraid, I forgot to live. No more."

Silence blanketed the drawing room.

"Well!" her mother said, looking frantically at her viscount.

Aunt Beatrice rustled on the chaise. "I have often remarked some indulgence of amusement should be granted to you, my dear niece, a picnic in Hyde Park would be acceptable and—"

"I've accepted an invitation to Lady Sterling's ball."

"You've received an invitation?" her mother gasped.

"A personally worded one," Emma said with a smile.

"Upon my word! Lady Sterling's ball is always held in town at her Mayfair mansion," her mother said, looking aghast. "Emma, dear, society will not be kind to you. Your limp is—"

"Has been my albatross and it will no longer be. If you are shamed by my attending, then I do not need to stay at our town house. I will procure myself a solicitor and proceed with letting a modest but suitable establishment while I am in London. I mean to experience a few of the delights of the town before I depart to visit Elizabeth. I am sure Boston society will be just as splendid, but it would be a grave sin if I did not have any tales to tell my sister of how wonderful the season in London has been."

Her family stared as if they could not understand her meaning, and Emma felt her heart breaking. Then Anthony stepped forward.

"We are not ashamed of you, Emma. We never have been, and we will never be."

Only Anthony seemed inclined to remark favorably, but she would be content with that.

"If you granted me the honor, I would be pleased to escort you to Lady Sterling's ball."

"Thank you," she mouthed, a film of tears blurring all their faces. Then unable to bear anymore questioning, she turned and left the room.

LADY STERLING's ball was a crush. It seemed to Emma the polite world was crammed into the wide-open ballroom. Almost an hour had passed, and no one had asked her to dance. She stood on the fringe of the ballroom, far away from the fashionable crowd, wishing for just a moment someone would brave society's censure and ask her to the floor. Instead, those who approached invariably withdrew after noting she stood with a walking cane.

After standing for a bit, Anthony had urged her to sit. Emma had refused, and she could feel the tension creeping into her muscles. Everyone stared. Pity and amusement shown in their gazes and the whispers rose like a swell across the ballroom. Dozens of fans flew opened, and ladies placed them in front of their mouths as if that would hide the knowledge from Emma that it was her they discussed.

What would Elliot do when he saw her? He was a duke, and appearances must be maintained. What had been his intention when he asked the hostess to send her an invitation? Dear God, what if she had misconstrued his intentions?

A sudden ripple through the crowd signaled that someone important had entered. Ladies craned their necks, and the whispering behind their fans rose. It was the duke and his grandmother. They descended the stairs and Emma stared helplessly at him. How terribly handsome he appeared dressed in dark jacket and trousers, with a golden waistcoat, a pristine white shirt, and a beautifully tied cravat. His hair had been recently trimmed, and no curls were present. In fact, he looked so austere, so ducal, and uncompromising, a little shiver of doubt went through her heart, yet the raw brilliance of his male beauty had pleasure darting through her. It then occurred to her this was the first time she observed him amongst his set.

Golden eyes scanned the crowd, and she waited, a thrill of sudden, intense excitement arrowing through her. She had taken such care with her appearance tonight. She had worn a gown of deep rose silk with an overskirt of silver gauze, white half gloves, and silver dancing slippers. Her short hair had been styled, and curls of hair puffed softly along her cheeks and forehead. Their gazes collided, and a hollowness formed in her stomach. There was no warm welcome, only cool, watchful reserve. No love shone from his gaze. She closed her eyes fleetingly as the realization struck.

Her heart thumped painfully, the urge to flee became overwhelming. Her fingernails dug stinging crescents into her palms. Uncertainty clawed at her stomach. Why had he sent gifts if he…?

As if her intentions were laid bare on her features, he extricated himself from his grandmother and prowled over to her. Several lords and ladies tried to capture his attention, but he was single mindedly concentrated in his regard. Which was definitely her.

He stopped a mere foot from her, if so much. "Miss Emma, will you honor me with a dance? And then perhaps allow me to escort you in for supper?"

She stared back at him with ill-concealed incredulity and wariness. "A dance?"

"Yes."

An unbearable tension wound itself around her heart. "Your Grace," she began, curtseying, keenly aware of a few ladies making no effort to hide their unashamed eavesdropping. She blinked back the moisture in her eyes. "I am not sure I can." The cane trembled in her arms.

"Would you like to try?" he asked in a deceptively mild tone.

His simple question, with no judgement in his eyes, had the tension seeping from her.

"And if I should stumble?"

"I'll catch you," he murmured, with a hint of gentleness and sensuality that sent flares of response racing through her.

"Forgive me for leaving you."

"Elliot?"

"I walked away when I should have fought for you…even if I was fighting you and your fears. I will never renew my offer to marry because my last offer still stands until you change your no into a yes. I will never marry another unless it is you. I'll wait on you for however long until you are ready, months, years, a lifetime. I know waiting will be a stark and lonely existence, but I know if it's not you, my life will forever be empty. For Emma…it has always been only you. I have known and loved you for ten years, with all your complexities and strength, with all your improper wildness, and this smile. And I will love you forever."

Someone gasped. Emma acted before she convinced herself to retreat. She turned around and leaned her walking cane along the wall, then she placed her hand in his, warmed by the approval which glowed in his eyes.

"You honor me, Emma."

The orchestra launched into a waltz, and her heart tripped. Then she was in his arms being glided across the floor. It was a bit disconcerting, to find herself on the dance floor rather than watching from the side of the ballroom. Everything felt off balance for precious moments, and then everything felt perfect. He was so graceful in his movements. Emma's heart tumbled in delight as he swept her in a wide arch, before pulling her close.

They danced for what felt like forever, but could only be a few minutes.

"God, you're beautiful," he murmured, admiration warmed in his eyes. "Your smile just now..."

She laughed, and then sobered as a shaft of pain arrowed up her leg and to her lower back. *Please, no.* The muscles tensed and slowly locked, and dread rose inside. She faltered, forcing him to stop in the middle of the ballroom, while other couples twirled around them.

"Fo... forgive me," she stammered.

She felt the weight of the guests' glares upon her. They were making no effort to be discreet.

Afraid to look at Elliot she tried to pull away and stumbled as a sharp cramp went through her legs. "Oh God."

Firm hands caught her, and she glanced up into golden eyes dark with concern…and love. A sob clawed from her throat. There was no shame, just a blinding love that had her trembling. Another sharp wrench of agony and she shook in reaction. "It hurts so much," she whispered, tears spilling down her cheek. How mortifying this would happen for all of society to witness.

And before all the duke of Hartford dropped to his knees before her, placed his hand under her ball gown and ran his strong fingers up to the muscles of her shin and up more to the flesh right above her knee.

"Hold on to my shoulders."

She complied. The scandalous impropriety of his actions had Emma's eyes widening. And remarkably a choked laugh escaped her when his grandmother fainted. The duke's action was tantamount to a proposal. How ridiculous it was that before all and sundry her reputation had just been compromised. But Emma hardly cared, the only thing that mattered was that the painful cramp was lessening as his delightful fingers kneaded the tight knots in her thighs. "It has eased," she whispered, quite aware that the room was silent.

How could they be so comfortable in their ogling she had no notion. Elliot removed his hands, careful that her ankles did not show. He stood, and with an imperious lift of his brow at the orchestra, music leaped to life. The very waltz they had been dancing.

"I fear you have been thoroughly compromised, to escape ruin we must either marry or flee to America. Would you like to continue dancing?"

She felt raw and exposed and terrified. She glanced up at him, aware that he was watching her closely, his gaze hooded, his body tensed. "Some days I feel pain so intense along my lower back and my legs I weep. I was such a mangled mess, Elliot. I have terrible scars, and on the best days, I still struggle with walking. You make me yearn for things that I'm certain I shouldn't want. A family. The hope for a child, some semblance of normalcy. I want to be strong enough to reach for the love I can see burning in your eyes, and I confess I feared you will regret your decision when the burden of my pain becomes too much to bear."

"You had such little faith in my love?"

"No…I had such little faith in me." Emerging

from that shattering awareness, she smiled, uncaring that tears were blurring her vision. "How I hate that we spent years apart. But now I see I needed that time to grow into the woman I am now. I am glad I did not marry you when I was hurt, broken and scared of simply living. I would have ruined us with my self-doubts and fear."

He brushed his thumb over her trembling lips. "I'll always be strong enough to carry you when you need me," he said solemnly. "And not because you are not capable enough, your strength humbles me and gives me hope for a future together. I love you with every part of me, Emma, and *nothing* could ever change that."

She stepped into his arms, and soared, her feet barely touching the ground, for he held most of her weight with his wonderful strength. Emma knew if she stumbled, his hands would be there, strong enough to catch her, powerful enough to hold her steady if she were to falter.

"I love you, Elliot, so desperately. I choose to marry, I am strong enough to believe in your love and to be your duchess. Marry me, Elliot. Be my lover, my friend, my husband, my duke."

His pleased laughter curled through her. And when she stumbled again, he paused, lifted her in his arms, and strode from the ballroom, uncaring of the scandal erupting in their wake. Nothing mattered to Emma at that moment either. Not the past, the fears, the scandal or what their future may hold. Just the present and the love and comfort she found in his arms. With a sigh of happiness, she rested her head on his shoulder.

They spilled into the night air, and he ordered the carriage. Elliot stood with her like that, and at odd times he would brush a kiss on her forehead. Suddenly she laughed, filled with bursting happiness and relief. "Elliot."

"I know," he murmured, and then remarkably he laughed too.

She was completed.

EPILOGUE

Their wedding night…

Less than two weeks after the *ton* declared themselves scandalized, Emma was the Duchess of Hartford. After so many years apart, to her family's distress, she had decided against a large wedding. Her duke had procured a special license, and they had wed in a small intimate ceremony in the chapel at Glenhaven House.

Hours after the wedding breakfast, they were ensconced in one of the most palatial bedchambers she had ever been in. Their room, for he had declared they would not have separate chambers, and she had happily agreed, was decorated with elegant carved mahogany furniture. The sofa and windows were covered with sweeping curtains in dark blue brocade velvet with silver trimming. A fireplace cast a golden sheen across her husband's magnificent body, and she stared at him with naked hunger and admiration.

How she had missed him while she counted the days until their wedding.

He pressed a kiss to the corner of her mouth, stroking the arousal he had already worked to a fever pitch in her body with his kisses, having licked places she did not know the names for and created wicked delight with his skillful fingers. Nerves thrummed through Emma as Elliot rolled down the white silken stockings and garter from her leg. Though she was secure in his love, the apprehension that he might find her deeply scarred leg repulsive enveloped her. Every other article of clothing had been removed from Emma, expect that lone stocking.

"Elliot," she whispered achingly as he untied her garters.

"Trust me?" he murmured.

She smiled. "Yes."

He rolled down her stocking, revealing the first long jagged scar that bisected her mid-thigh and down to her knees. He stroked her skin absently with his fingers, the gesture was more soothing than words. Then he continued down, peeling back the stocking slowly, revealing more rough, twisted flesh. Her shin and calf were roped with twisted scars, the ridges rough and unseemly. He tenderly kissed the rough edges and removed her stocking in full.

He glanced up, and the love and sorrow in his eyes eased the tension inside.

"You'll never need me again, and find I'm not there. You will always have me at your side."

He pushed her back onto the large four poster bed, covering her body like a warm, sensual blanket. They kissed tenderly…and deeply. The dark, rich taste of him enveloped her senses, and with gasps and moans and affirmations of love, Emma and Elliot had a glorious wedding night.

One year later…

Emma smiled down at the contented baby in her arms. Julian Alexander Winthrop, the Marquess of Ashbrook and the future Duke of Hartford, was only a few minutes old, but she already loved him with her entire soul. He had a shock of dark unruly hair and the face of a Botticelli cherub, she could not imagine a more beautiful baby.

"Look at him, Elliot," she said awe and tears roughing her voice, all the pain and discomfort of the last few months and hours forgotten.

Everything had been worth holding this precious bundle in her arms, even those last six weeks when she had been confined to bed. Not that it had been overly ghastly, the lack of activity had simply been hard to bear, but her duke had spent every day with her, reading, playing chess, painting together, and explaining to her about his business investments.

Emma had thought her happiness could not increase, but now…

"Look at his little, pink, wrinkled face. He is perfect and so handsome. Oh, Elliot, he will break many hearts," she said with a watery laugh.

"If you believe so, my love," her husband said indulgently.

There was no description to express the love and happiness pouring through her heart. "We are truly blessed aren't we, my darling?"

"Indeed, we are, my love. Indeed we are."

THANK you for reading **The Duke and I**!

I hope you enjoyed the journey to happy ever after for Elliot and Emma. **REVIEWS ARE GOLD TO AUTHORS,** for they are a very important part of reaching readers, and I do hope you will consider leaving an honest review on Amazon adding to my rainbow. It does not have to be lengthy, a simple sentence or two will do. Just know that I will appreciate your efforts sincerely.

CONTINUE READING FOR A SNEAK PEEK INTO THE NEXT BOOK OF THE SERIES

THE VISCOUNT AND I

Forever Yours Series Book 3

Excerpt

Grab a Copy Today

After jilting first a fortune hunter, then a lying libertine, Lady Fanny Dashwood has given up on marrying for love. This time it will be strictly business – a man who'll agree to her terms, give her the children she craves, but will not trouble her heart.

Sebastian Rutledge, Viscount Shaw, has desired Lady Fanny from afar for years. However, he is a factory owner with a new title – not nearly good enough for an earl's daughter. Until a dream opportunity arises: a marriage of convenience with the woman of his dreams. Even as their growing passion unleashes in the bedchamber, his new wife remains at arm's length. Could a wellborn lady ever fall for an unconventional lord?

CHAPTER ONE

Hanover Square, London

I'm to be married, finally.

A fierce joy sparkled inside Lady Frances Elizabeth Dashwood, Fanny to her close friends and family. Her dear mamma had long despaired this day would ever come, considering Fanny had been the cause of a most dreadful scandal several years past. A disgrace that had sent her papa to his grave, or so her mother, the dowager countess often lamented, even though Papa had died four months after the unfortunate incident.

It had taken years, three to be precise before Fanny had been tentatively enfolded back into the bosom of society. How glorious it had been this season to finally attend balls, musicales, and ride through Hyde Park once more, without ladies lifting their fans and cutting her, without speculative whispers, and the dreadful conversations that abruptly ended whenever she approached. Of course, being courted by Harry Basil, the Marquess of Trent had been the feather needed to set her cap upright.

And today they were tying the knot at St. George's, Hanover Square. Determined to look ravishing, she'd worn a fashionable dress of the palest pink silk, which accentuated her curvy figure to its best advantage. She'd caught her blonde hair up in the most elegant of chignons with becoming wisps framing her face, and a coronet of flowers woven between the strands. Today was to be a most splendid day, and Fanny ensured she appeared the most elegant and perfect bride.

The ceremony was to start in fifteen minutes. Her carriage had already driven around the square a number of times because her mother was so eager that her daughter had landed a gentleman of such esteem, but it would not do for her to be waiting in the church on him. Her mother was glowing with pleasure at the prospective match. Fanny thought it absurd but had agreed to remain in the carriage until the marquess reached the altar. She had done so to settle her mother's nerves. Fanny had never been one to display emotions of any sorts in public, and she had needed a few moments to herself.

Her carriage paused at the grand frontage of St. George's and a footman jumped down to confirm whether the Marquess had arrived. Apparently, his carriage had delivered him on her previous circuit of the square. Her step was let down, and she was helped down by the footman. She smiled at him nervously as she straightened her shoulders to climb the steps to the entrance. It was hard not to be intimidated by the imposing façade with its six Doric pillars and Grecian triangular frieze. Her mother in the second carriage would organize the bridesmaids and follow her up. Her brother Colin, the current Earl of Banberry should be waiting in the porch for her and then they would proceed up the central aisle on the red carpet to the altar.

She opened the church door and entered, taking a left turn down an isolated corridor. She faltered as she spied a couple ahead. The man appeared familiar. Something terrible and fearful gripped Fanny's heart and a cold knot twisted through her stomach. For precious seconds she was unable to comprehend the sight. The man she was to marry was locked in the most passionate of embraces with a lady Fanny recognized as Miss Miranda Shelby.

Fanny only had cause to know Miss Shelby for she had been the unfortunate recipient of vulgar rumors which claimed Lord Trent had offered this woman *carte blanche*. She had asked her brother for clarification, and he had refused to mortify her sensibilities. Against her brother's advice, she had asked her betrothed about Miss Shelby, and the marquess had re-assured Fanny, his friendship with Miss Shelby was in the past.

The hot sting of tears burned her eyes. The loving way he placed her palm on his cheek and the tender smile on his lips belied his assurances and promises given only last week. A crushing weight settled against her chest, and an alarming sound of pain slipped from her. The two lovers were too enthralled with their moment, to notice Fanny hovering on the threshold.

"Oh, my darling, I cannot bear that you are to be married. How I despair I will lose you," Miss Shelby cried, crushing the marquess's hand to her chest. Her bosom heaved over her low-cut gown, her golden ringlets bobbed with her agitation, and Fanny suspected the lady's light blue eyes glistened with tears.

"You will never lose me," Lord Trent vowed fervently. "As soon as possible my sweeting, I will order Lady Fanny to the country, and she will remain there until I say otherwise. Nothing will sway my love for you…" Then he lowered his hand to the gentle protrusion under her gown. "I will be with you every step of the way when our babe comes into this world."

They kissed fiercely, their ardor for each other mortifying, and an arrow of envy and sorrow darted through Fanny's heart. She desperately wanted to flee, but her limbs would not obey her. She was frozen, the pain hammering through her terribly. Lord Trent had professed to love her, had showered her with acceptable gifts, and had even stolen a few kisses, a liberty she had allowed for she had been so sure she loved him in return.

All evidence showed he was ardently caught in the throes of passion with Miss Miranda Shelby. The few indelicate rumors Fanny had heard, could no longer be denied. She turned away, a harsh sob tearing from her throat, and hurried down the hallway. Tears blurred her vision and hating the notion the marquess might exit and see her fleeing, she clutched the skirts of her dress and ran.

"Fanny?"

With a gasp she halted, pressing trembling

fingers to her lips. "Mamma..." How she wished she could fling herself into her mother's arms.

"My dear girl, you are fleeing as if the devil is on your heel. It is not seemly." The countess glanced behind Fanny, her elegant brows puckered in a severe frown.

She allowed her mother to tug her toward a hidden alcove near the entrance that would lead her to the altar.

"What is amiss, Fanny?"

She desperately tried to swallow past the pain in her throat. "Lord Trent..."

"Yes?"

A flush traveled along her body. "I saw him just now, clasped in a most improper embrace with Miss Shelby."

Her mother considered her as if she had never seen her before. "And this is what has you so out of sorts?"

Confusion rushed through Fanny. "Mamma, they...they were declaring passionate love for each other, and kissing most salaciously," she whispered, beyond mortified to be revealing such intimacy to her mother.

"Pish. Today is a most auspicious day, and the only thing that is important is in a few minutes you will be a countess. Lady Trent. The likes of Miranda Shelby should never upset you. She is too low to be given any prominence in our thoughts. Now let's set you to rights, for the ceremony is to start."

Fanny grappled for a precious moment to perceive her meaning. "Mamma, I cannot marry a man who has no regard for me, and on the day we are to marry he is professing his devotion—"

"Nonsense," her mother said sharply, her dark green eyes flashing with ire and determination. "Men will always flatter their vanity and have their mistresses. It's the way of the world, and we do not let it bother us. As ladies, there are far more pressing matters to occupy our attention."

Fanny recoiled. "You are speaking in jest, of course! The fidelity and the honor of the man I marry cannot be suspect. Mamma—"

Her mother gripped her chin in a painful clasp, shocking Fanny into silence.

"You will listen to me, Fanny Elizabeth Dashwood. You were foolish enough to break your betrothal to Viscount Aldridge because it was revealed it was your fortune which attracted him. It took years for society to forgive your outrageous behavior. You are on the cusp of being a marchioness, and you will not ruin your chances and bring disgrace to this family again."

Disgrace.

She trembled at the reminder of how intolerably unforgiving society had been when she had rejected the viscount weeks after her initial acceptance of his proposal. She made no reply, for Fanny was a mess with the emotions rioting so forcefully inside.

"Gather your composure, we have a wedding to attend."

Then her brother appeared from inside the church, and she was hustled down the aisle on his arm so that he could give her away.

Several minutes later, Fanny stood at the altar of the cathedral, facing the marquess, who did not have the appearance of a man who had been passionately making love to another. He peered down at her with familiar tenderness. She had been so confident he loved her. Was she so naïve and desperate for a family she had allowed a libertine to deceive her? How could she have been so mistaken in his heart and character?

Colin stated that he was giving her away before taking his seat.

The bishop began the ceremony, and she bit the

inside of her bottom lip to prevent the tears burning behind her eyes from spilling over.

"Dearly beloved, we are gathered together here in the sight of God, and in the face of this congregation, to join together this man and this woman in holy matrimony; which is an honorable estate…"

Please stop talking! It would not do to be fodder for gossip on her wedding day. Nor must she bring disgrace to her family. Lifting her chin, she squared her shoulders and met the gaze of the man she would pledge to love and obey for the rest of her life. He winked, a charming habit he had whenever he wanted to make her smile. But now she saw the emptiness and the lies for what it was. He did not love or esteem her, it had all been a cruel charade with a purpose she could not understand. The earl did not desire her fortune, for society knew he commanded fifty thousand pounds a year. It *hadn't* been because she was an heiress.

Lord Trent had courted her so ardently with the sweetest of poems and flowers. All those long walks in the park, the picnics, and the dancing at balls. They had meant nothing to him for his plan was to send her to the country, while he resided in passionate bliss with the woman he loved. Fanny trembled, and Lord Trent frowned, concern darkening his eyes. *Liar*, she wanted to snarl, hating that she was reduced to this mess of pain and anxiety on a day she had been anticipating since her sixteenth birthday.

"Henry George Basil, Marquess of Trent, wilt thou have Lady Frances Elizabeth Dashwood to thy wedded wife, to live together after God's ordinance in the holy estate of matrimony? Wilt thou love her, comfort her, honor, and keep her in sickness and in health; and, forsaking all other, keep thee only unto her, so long as ye both shall live?

"I do."

It was becoming more difficult to breathe by the minute.

Fanny perceived she was poised on the cusp of the scandal of the season. She would make everyone forget the jubilation of their beloved Queen Victoria's coronation, and last week's disgrace of Sebastian Rutledge—the Iron King—in refusing to marry Miss Arabella Sutton, despite being caught in a compromising situation with the lady. No, Fanny's scandal would be like no other.

The slice of pain that went through her heart made her tremble. *I will lose everything I have been hoping for.* To marry this man after what she had witnessed…

"Lady Frances Elizabeth Dashwood, wilt thou have this man to thy wedded husband, to live together after God's ordinance in the holy estate of matrimony? Wilt thou obey him, and serve him, love, honor, and keep him in sickness and in health; and, forsaking all other, keep thee only unto him, so long as ye both shall live?"

A dreadful silence blanketed the church as the bishop waited for her affirmation. Why had she allowed herself to be persuaded to the altar? A murmur of voices penetrated her panicked thoughts, and her gaze snapped to the dozens of guests in attendance. Only one hundred or so people were present to witness the joining, but it felt as if all of society waited in judgment. If she did not commit now…if she truly walked away, she would be *ruined*, and nothing would render her respectable.

The knot in her throat was growing.

Her mother paled and gripped her brother's arm who seemed to observe something was wrong. Colin slowly stood, his hands clenching at his side, a warning flashing in his expression.

The bishop cleared his throat the action shaking his jowls.

"Lady Fanny, is all well?" Lord Trent asked, peering down at her.

"I saw you," she finally answered. Her throat felt thick, and there was a tightness across her chest that made it difficult to breathe. "I saw you…with your mistress." A woman who also waited in the pews. How did she dare stand watching the man she loved marrying another? Humiliation clawed through Fanny at the memory of how they had clung to each other only a few moments ago, and the whispered words of promises her fiancé had vowed.

The Marquess stiffened, knowledge darkening his pale blue eyes. He reached for her gloved fingers, and to the onlooker, his clasp would have seemed gentle. But her fingers ached from the way he subtly twisted them. She tried to yank her fingers back, but there was no give in the marquess's grip.

Something awful must lurk within her, for she knew to walk away would be the ruination of all her dreams and the reputation she had struggled to reclaim. Fanny desperately wanted her own family. She was three and twenty and after the last fiasco three seasons ago when she had called off her engagement to viscount Aldridge, the scandal had been terrible. The viscount had even threatened to sue her family for breach of promise, and her father had settled an unnamed sum on him. The scandal sheet had dubbed her the runaway heiress, and for the longest time, Fanny had thought society would never accept her back again.

But they had, and she had crept from the shell she had slipped under to protect herself from their vicious gossiping, and cruel scrutiny. If she did not marry the marquess now…everything she had wanted for so very long would disappear like ashes with the wind.

Lord Trent lowered his head. "You will confirm your vows," he warned, twisting her fingers, grinding the knuckles against each other.

A low whimper escaped her, and her heart quaked. Another revelation flowed through her soul. Not only was he a libertine who planned to order her to the country and be wicked with his mistress, but he was also cruel. This was a man who would not hesitate to beat her if she should dare defy him. How could she have been so mistaken in his character?

"You will release me, or I shall scream."

He ignored her, and Fanny slapped him. His

expression of comical dismay filled her with satisfaction. Then she walked away unable to look into the faces of her guests, especially her dearest friends and close family. With every step she felt the awful weight of their shock and judgment. Eyes followed her, the whispers of shock accumulating and cresting in a swell through the church. The news would spread through society like wildfire, and her family might never forgive her. The scandal sheets would burn for weeks with this spectacle.

Unable to walk serenely down the aisle, she ran.

WANT TO KNOW WHAT HAPPENS NEXT?

CONTINUE READING...

FREE OFFER

SIGN UP TO MY NEWSLETTER TO CLAIM YOUR FREE BOOK!

To claim your FREE copy of Wicked Deeds on a Winter Night, a delightful and sensual romp to indulge in your reading addiction, please click here.

Once you've signed up, you'll_be among the first to hear about my new releases, read excerpts you won't find anywhere else, and patriciate in subscriber's only giveaways and contest. I send out on dits once a month and on super special occasion I might send twice, and please know you can unsubscribe whenever we no longer zing.

Happy reading!

Stacy Reid

ACKNOWLEDGMENTS

I thank God every day for my family, friends, and my writing. A special thank you to my husband. I love you so hard! Without your encouragement and steadfast support I would not be living my dream of being an author. You encourage me to dream and are always steadfast in your wonderful support. You read all my drafts, offer such amazing insight and encouragement. Thank you for designing my fabulous cover! Thank you for reminding me I am a warrior when I wanted to give up on so many things.

Thank you, Giselle Marks for being so wonderful and supportive always. You are a great critique partner and friend. Readers, thank you for giving me a chance and reading my book! I hope you enjoyed and would consider leaving a review. Thank you!

ABOUT STACY

USA Today Bestselling author Stacy Reid writes sensual Historical and Paranormal Romances and is the published author of over twenty books. Her debut novella The Duke's Shotgun Wedding was a 2015 HOLT Award of Merit recipient in the Romance Novella category, and her bestselling Wedded by Scandal series is recommended as Top picks at Night Owl Reviews, Fresh Fiction Reviews, and The Romance Reviews.

Stacy lives a lot in the worlds she creates and actively speaks to her characters (aloud). She has a warrior way "Never give up on dreams!" When she's not writing, Stacy spends a copious amount of time binge-watching series like The Walking Dead, Altered Carbon, Rise of the Phoenixes, Ten Miles of Peach Blosson, and playing video games with her love. She also has a weakness for ice cream and will have it as her main course.

Stacy is represented by Jill Marsal at Marsal Lyon Literary Agency.

She is always happy to hear from readers and would love to connect with you via my Website, Facebook, and Twitter. To be the first to hear about her new releases, get cover reveals, and excerpts you won't find anywhere else, sign up for her newsletter, or join her over at Historical Hellions, her fan group!

Follow me on BookBub

Printed by Amazon Italia Logistica S.r.l.
Torrazza Piemonte (TO), Italy

15398800R00137